HeartBeat

A Sci-Fi, Tragi-Comedic, Rock 'n' Roll Fantasy
Screen Book

By
Matthew Wolfe

THIS BOOK HAS BEEN RATED PG-13
by The Samuel Wolfe Screen Book Association,
though it may deserve an R or even X rating,
depending on your imagination.

Based on
HeartBeat, the 2001 novel
By Matthew Wolfe

Published by:
Samuel Wolfe Books
6 Maple Drive
Huntington, WV 25705

Editor: Melissa Shepherd
Assistant Editor: Brian Bellomy
Charitable Marketing Director: Katie Wolfe

For additional information ,
Visit: mysticalwolfe.weebly.com
wolfem@ohio.edu

ISBN: 978-0-9995196-2-2

Font: We spent minutes deciding that we should use the `Courier font` throughout this book (except this legal stuff) to give the reader the added thrill of a text that looks like it came from an old typewriter at 3 in the am while the writer was trashed. You are welcome.

Printed in the U.S.A.

In memory of
my Bonus Mom,
Mary Sue Dameron.
She greatly loved this
whacky story.
-- And me, too.

Why Watch A Book
When You Can Read The Movie?

Authors do not supply imaginations.
They expect their readers to have
their own, and to use it. - Nella Larsen

So, I wrote a screenplay. Yay.

Maybe you did, too.

This year alone, I and 1,257,362 other hacks thought we could write a script better than half the crap we see on the tiny screens at our local multiplex. We gambled. We threw the dice. We spun the wheel. Even as our sheer numbers made the chance of seeing our scripts come to fruition at least 500,000 to 1.

Even worse, I live in West Virginia. Exactly 2300 miles separate my desk from the famous Hollywood sign. I have zero connections in the film industry. Watch the odds stack up against me.

Oh, and there's a new option for aspiring screenwriters: "Make a Pitch Trailer!" This is how speculation (spec.) scripts get sold to producers these days, according to half the spam in my email inbox, all of it selling how-to guides for making the so-called "Pitch Trailer". But I'm too lazy and broke to film a commercial tease for my scripts. I'd rather sit in my big chair and bitch about the hard life of a writer.

And once a year, I spend Oscar Night sitting in my big chair bitching about how awards for the arts breed homogenous work instead encouraging originality - even as I think that taking home a statue could be great fun. Just imagine how cool my acceptance speech would be.

During the Oscars, I drink whiskey, eat cookies, and post my witticisms on Facebook so that my words are reaching SOMEBODY out there. I post things like: "If you wear a shirt with your favorite movie quote on it, is that clothes captioning?"

Seriously, my acceptance speech would rock.

REALITY CHECK

The odds of my script becoming a major motion picture are less than that of a toad hitching a cross-country ride on the back of an eagle so that he might dine on seventeen-foot Alaskan mosquitos.

Still, in spite of these odds, I have a unique story to tell, a story I like very much. I have art to share! And this is America, damn it all. I need to sell, sell, sell my soul — I mean, my idea. I helped *create* the modern DYI sensibility! This is what Print On Demand (POD) publishing was made for! I'll just self-publish my little script, send it into the world, and see where it winds up. Even better, I'll break a lot of script writing rules to make it more accessible to the average reader. Who doesn't love breaking rules?

Thus my concept for the Screen Book was born. This is *not* a spec. script or a treatment. It is *not* a shooting script, a post-theatrical release fan script, or a novelization. It is a vision script: this is what I see in my head when I sit back and imagine what my story should look like on a big screen while I clutch my tub of popcorn, box of Junior Mints, and a tankard of soda.

This is a Screen Book.

MUSIC IS EVERYTHING

One rule I often see in the scriptwriting books is that the writer should NEVER make music suggestions. That's the job of the director and music director. So I dutiful mashed over 15 song titles into the *HeartBeat* Screen Book. I mean, I blew that rule out of the swamp!

Music has been integral to my life for over 50 years. How can I *not* think of possibilities while writing? Here, I gave myself free license and let my imagination run like a player piano.

During the various rewrites, something different emerged. My song choices matched the story so well that I began to see the scenes as music videos. By my estimation, there could be as many as 67 minutes of well-known rock songs and instrumentals blasting from the theater speakers. The other 50 minutes just link the music videos together.

So download your own version of the soundtrack/playlist (see Appendix B), plug in your ears, and listen while you read. And would someone please let me know just how many times the word "heart" pops up in these songs? Thank You.

PRODUCTION POTENTIAL

This is not the craziest thing I have ever written, but it is the craziest one to see the light of day. Now if it became a flickering light on a silver screen, that would be even better. My ego wants to see the movie made. It's only natural I suppose. I would love to see the word "HeartBeat" in lights over the entrance to the big, old movie palace in my hometown.

And just as soon as a major studio offers me a check for $500,000, a guarantee of %50 of the royalties, and a production budget of $99 million (anything more would self-indulgent), that's just what will happen. Right?

No way. The sun will blow up, vaporize the earth, and make aliens peering through their telescopes say, "Oh" and "Ah," as they view the galactic fireworks long before my movie gets made that way.

Still, if someone really wants to irritate enough electrons to "film" this madness, I'm open to other possibilities (and significantly less money).

Maybe someone would like to make it look like a 1950s,
B-movie: film it in black and white with intentionally
bad (cheap) special effects. It could be a flickering
tribute to early sci-fi movies and drive-in theaters.

Or maybe *HeartBeat* should be animated or brought to
life with Claymation! Maybe puppetry would do the
trick. Maybe you have a new idea. Have your people
call my people. We'll do lunch.

Or, to be even more realistic: If you like this story
and my vision for the film, let's play "Six Degrees of
Steven Spielberg." You know someone who knows someone
who knows someone with real clout in the film industry.
Pass this Screen Book along that chain of elbow
rubbing. If it all works out, you, too, can watch your
name go by at 60 mph in tiny print in the "Much Thanks"
section of the final credits. Wouldn't that be great?
Hell, I'd buy your ticket. Get it the hands of
Spielberg himself, and I'll take you to the Oscars when
it's nominated for best screenplay.

After all, a guy's gotta dream.
- MWolfe, Winter 2018

ABBREVIATIONS KEY

Most people already know or figure out the many
abbreviations used in scripts, but here is a little
guide to get you started.

INT - Interior Scene
EXT - Exterior Scene
IN/OUT - Film this scene at an In-N-Out Burger joint

POV - Point of View
O.C. - Actor off camera
O.S. - Actor off screen
O.M. - Actor off medications

NAME (CONT'D) - Character continues speaking after some
directions are made.

(BEAT) - A short pause in the dialog.
(V.O.) - Voice over.
ANGLE ON - Camera direction to focus on a specific item
or person.

MUSIC CONT. - Music continues from one section to the
        next.
XYZ - Examine Your Zipper before standing in front of a
camera.

WARNING!

If you are an aspiring screenwriter, toss this script-like platypus back
into the bargain-books bin. NOW! If you use this book as a model to
format or write a screenplay, it will *bite* you. Why? A) I have no idea
what I am doing. B) This is screen BOOK – a hybrid genre I have
created for my own amusement. You Have Been Warned.

Have a Nice Day,
-- MWolfe

The Loco Lobo Theater now has
Clothes Captioned™ T-shirts For HeartBeat!

I just wanted to be
left alone.
                    -- Ethan
         or

Oh Honey, that's just
the explosives talking.
                    -- Karen

Just $29.99 in the theater lobby.

****

Wednesday nights are
Whiskey Wednesday Nites
At the Loco Lobo Bar,
conveniently located next door.
Fill a flask before the show.
The ushers won't look.

****

The producers of tonight's
feature, *HeartBeat*,
Wish to remind you to sign
your organ donor card.

"Save a life.
Have the adventure of a lifetime."

****

At this time the management
Of Loco Lobo Theater asks you to
turn off your phone,
grab the popcorn, and settle
back in your favorite big chair.

And now. Turn the page for our

FEATURE PRESENTATION

HEARTBEAT

In your heart,
you can hear another
human scream.

<u>HeartBeat</u>

CUE the ethereal opening of Aerosmith's "Sweet Emotion."

FADE IN ON:

EXT.   SOLAR SYSTEM, NEAR EARTH

Our POV (Point of View) is as though we have been impaled on the nose of a fast-moving spaceship or missile. We hurtle toward EARTH at a terrifying speed. The North Pole is at the bottom. The planet is "up-side-down"(there is no "up" or "down" in zero gravity).

EARTH grows in size as we zip closer at nearly the speed of light. We spin and turn until we can make out the east coast of North America at the top of the screen.

EARTH fills the screen. Our POV shudders and rattles as we charge into the atmosphere. Flames flare up before us. There is enough air for us to hear sounds again. Horrible RATTLING noises now compete with "Sweet Emotion."

The US mid-Atlantic region fills the middle of the screen, as the flames shuffle off to the sides. The vibrations and RATTLING smooth out. Our sensation shifts: it now appears that we are sitting still and the EARTH is rushing up to us. Instead slowing, everything accelerates. Washington DC is rushing up to us. City blocks and streets grow in an instant. Cars and people pop up in unison.

We are going to crash!

We plunge into an intersection just as two cars are about to collide. We will hit the cars just as they hit each other.

BRAKES squeal. Everything lurches to a halt. We are about two feet from two fenders that are inches apart.

1

One fender is blue, the other black.

The MUSIC, "Sweet Emotion," continues.

The camera gently pans along the side of the black car, a mint-condition, 1988 Crown Victoria.

The camera pauses on the driver, RICHARD HAMLIN, a middle-aged white man with blue eyes. He is stoic.

RICHARD calmly lights a cigarette with the car's lighter while we hear the other driver SHOUTING cusswords. After a couple of puffs, Richard casually gives the other driver the middle finger.

The camera now flows in through the driver's side window. It turns as it passes between RICHARD's face and hand gesture, so that we see the ANGRY MAN through the windshield.

We also see an old HIPPIE/DUDE walking through the scene. He stoops to pick up something between the cars, but we can't see what it is.

As the camera moves, we see RICHARD's finger and pass on toward the passenger side. The SHOUTING fades out, but the MUSIC continues.

The camera pans down to the passenger seat and angles on a dark blue windbreaker with the letters FBI on it. Beside the letters, a blue butterfly with red eyes and spots rests on the jacket.

The butterfly rises, turns, and flies through the open passenger window.

We follow the butterfly through:

EXT. Washington, D.C. – Day

ROLL OPENING CREDITS AS "SWEET EMOTION" CONTINUES.

We see a series of shots of the butterfly at famous D.C. landmarks: flitting by the Viet Nam War Memorial, sitting on the shoulder of a statue at Korean War Memorial, fluttering by the sign to the Holocaust Museum, landing for a break on Lincoln's knee at the Lincoln Memorial, amusing a child in a park, and so forth.

Then, as the credits finish, the butterfly flits across a street in a residential neighborhood where it is suddenly splattered on the grill of a black, 2017 Cadillac Escalade.

END MUSIC.

Fade to Black.

INT. ABANDONED DC PARKING GARAGE - DAY

RICHARD HAMLIN stands near his car on the first level.

RICHARD takes a deep draw on a Camel cigarette then drops it to the pavement.

ANGLE ON: The "Camel" logo as RICHARD crushes it with the toe of his shiny, black shoe.

Tires SQUEAL as a black Escalade pulls up about 15 feet from Richard.

ANGLE ON the splattered butterfly on the Escalade's grill. One wing is still twitching. The eyes glow red.

The camera zooms in. We see tiny wires, springs, and a tiny motherboard. Electricity arcs across the pieces, and the eyes go dark. The butterfly was a robot.

CUT TO:

STANLEY, a large white man with a shaved head, steps out from the driver's side.

RICHARD frowns, slowly reaches for the gun in his shoulder holster.

DREADS, an Arabic man with dreadlocks, emerges from the shadows behind RICHARD. He places a straight razor at RICHARD's throat.

RICHARD sighs and raises his hands slightly while
STANLEY approaches him and relieves him of his gun.

STANLEY opens the back door of the Escalade. Out pops
AHAB, an Iranian man in an Armani suit.

AHAB steps toward RICHARD.

                    AHAB
          Ah. Richard Hamlin, the FBI's
          problem child.

                    RICHARD
          And you are?

                    AHAB
          Your bosses call me Ahab.

                    RICHARD
          And the informant?

                    AHAB
          He was on his way to see you,
          so we gave him a ride.
          Stanley?

STANLEY opens the back of the SUV, drags out a gagged
and bound white TEENAGER with track marks from
shooting up heroin on his arms. STANLEY drags him to
the center. The TEENAGER looks up at RICHARD with
pleading eyes.

                    RICHARD
          (To TEENAGER) Sorry, kid.

                    AHAB
          (To DREADS) Get your toy.

DREADS steps away from RICHARD.

                    RICHARD
          (To AHAB) What do you want?

                    AHAB
          Your death.

                    RICHARD
          Then let the kid go.

                    AHAB
          I'm afraid that's no longer
          possible.

DREADS reappears near the TEENAGER. DREADS has a

4

crossbow and aims it at the TEENAGER'S head.

                    RICHARD
          You want me to talk?

                    AHAB
          Talk? (Chuckles) Christ,
          Richard, I know more than you
          do.

AHAB nods to DREADS.

DREADS pulls the trigger. The bolt (arrow) goes
through the TEENAGER's head. The TEENAGER slumps over.

                    AHAB (CONT'D)
          (To RICHARD) You see
          Richard, I provide special
          services for your bosses. In
          return, I import all the
          heroin I can, and they look
          the other way. It's a very
          cozy arrangement. But you do
          not play well with others, my
          friend. And so, they -- we
          want you out of the way.

                    RICHARD
          Why would anyone in the FBI
          go to such lengths for you?

                    AHAB
          They use my "donations" to
          fund a top-secret program.
          Then, when I have enough men
          and resources, I will return
          to Iran, destroy that
          goddamned fundamentalist
          regime, and turn the nukes
          over to the US.

Pause.

                    AHAB (CONT'D)
          Yes. I can almost see the
          pieces of the puzzle fall
          together in your head. And
          now you know you have been
          set up.

                    RICHARD
          What's your end game?

                    AHAB
         I will be Iran's new
         president.

                    RICHARD
         Proud dreams are for naive
         souls to ponder.

                    AHAB

         Oh. A poet. Well. You'll have
         plenty to ponder in hell,
         Richard Hamlin. (To DREADS)
         Dreads.

DREADS aims the crossbow and a fresh bolt at RICHARD's
head. RICHARD and DREADS stare each other down.

Just as DREADS squeezes the trigger, RICHARD turns
around and launches himself across the hood of his
car.

DREADS jerks the trigger. The bolt plants itself in
the front fender, just inches from RICHARD'S head.

                    STANLEY
         Told you shotguns are better.

RICHARD slips to the floor on the opposite side of his
car and runs for a nearby stairway door.

STANLEY draws a gun and takes two shots at RICHARD.
Both miss. RICHARD scrambles through the door.

                    AHAB
         (To Stanley) Follow him up
         the stairs. (To Dreads) You,
         take his car. Run him down if
         you have to, but finish him
         off with the crossbow. That's
         our brand now.

INT. STAIRWELL - DAY

MUSIC: "The Main Monkey Business" by Rush

RICHARD crouches, draws a German Mauser-7,65 pistol
from his ankle holster. He then rushes up the stairs.

STANLEY enters the stairwell. They take several shots
at each other. STANLEY takes a slug in the knee.

                       6

                    STANLEY
               Oh! Mother of God!

INT. PARKING GARAGE/LEVEL TWO - DAY

MUSIC CONT.

RICHARD bursts through a door with a big "2" painted
on it. He looks around then runs for a fire escape.

RICHARD hears the ROAR and SQUEAL of his own car
coming up the ramp for him. He runs faster. The car
gains.

RICHARD rolls off to the side just as the car is about
to run him down.

DREADS deftly spins the car around to face RICHARD.
RICHARD is boxed in by walls.

DREADS ROARS toward RICHARD. RICHARD fires shots and
runs toward the car. Bullets strike and shatter the
windshield.

RICHARD belly flops onto the hood, aims at DREADS,
pulls the trigger. CLICK. Empty. RICHARD tosses the
gun.

DREADS grins and throws the car into reverse. RICHARD
begins to slide off and grabs a windshield wiper.

DREADS whips the car around then heads for a ramp to
level three.

AHAB comes in behind driving the SUV.

STANLEY staggers through the Level Two door just in
time to see everyone leave.

                    STANLEY (To himself)
               I hate Mondays.

INT. PARKING GARAGE/LEVEL THREE - DAY

MUSIC CONT.

DREADS erratically swerves the car to throw RICHARD.
RICHARD's legs dangle off one side.

RICHARD pulls the crossbow bolt out of the fender and
tries to stab DREADS through the shattered windshield.

DREADS sideswipes a wall, smashes RICHARD's legs.

DREADS aims the car for a pile of rusty old paint cans someone has dumped here.

BOOM. Paint cans crash everywhere. Peach paint sprays and streams over the black car [Yes, English Teachers. It's symbolic Colonization Brand paint.]

RICHARD tosses the bolt to grab the frame of the broken windshield. Blood wells up around his fingers.

AHAB, behind, swerves the limo around the paint mess.

DREADS grabs a paint can that has landed in the car and bashes RICHARD'S face and hands with it.

The cars ROAR up to level four, the open-air top of the garage.

EXT. PARKING GARAGE/TOP LEVEL - DAY

MUSIC CONT.

In desperation, RICHARD tries to swing around to the open, driver's side window.

DREADS tosses the paint can, pulls out his straight razor.

RICHARD tries to reach in, but DREADS slashes his arms and face with deep cuts. Blood flows.

RICHARD loses his grip and falls away from the car.

AHAB aims the SUV at RICHARD. RICHARD tries to stand on his broken legs.

Just as RICHARD falls again, the grill of the SUV (with the butterfly robot) strikes him and hurls him across the concrete.

RICHARD struggles to get up, but he is too damaged. The shadows of DREADS and AHAB fall on his broken body.

> AHAB
> (To DREADS) Drag him to his
> car. Prop him up in the
> driver's seat.

DREADS does as ordered. AHAB strolls to the front of

RICHARD'S peach and black car.

STANLEY staggers up to AHAB.

                    AHAB (CONT'D)
               (To STANLEY) Where have you
               been?

                    STANLEY
               I got shot! In the fuckin'
               knee!

                    AHAB
               Whatever. (To DREADS)
               That's good. And tie the
               seatbelt around him, so he
               can't wiggle out.

DREADS secures RICHARD then retrieves his crossbow
from the backseat.

DREADS joins AHAB and STANLEY.

RICHARD, nearly dead, looks at his dashboard. The
tachometer needle twitches slightly. The engine is
still running.

                    AHAB (CONT.)
               (To RICHARD) You put up a
               good fight, Richard Hamlin,
               but not good enough.

RICHARD summons his remaining strength to put his hand
on the gear selector and his foot over the gas pedal.

DREADS aims to put a bolt through the hole in the
windshield and between RICHARD'S eyes.

AHAB pulls out his iPhone to shoot video.

                    AHAB (CONT'D)
               This'll make great
               advertising.

RICHARD drops the gear into D and floors the pedal.

DREADS jerks the shot again. The bolt hits RICHARD'S
neck.

DREADS and AHAB rush out of the way, but with a bullet
in his knee, STANLEY isn't so lucky.

RICHARD'S car strikes STANLEY and shoves him into the
low, outer wall of the garage.

9

The old concrete crumbles. STANLEY, RICHARD, and the car plunge to the street below. CRASH!

AHAB and DREADS peer over the edge in disbelief. They hear a SIREN in the distance. They run for the SUV.

EXT. PARKING GARAGE EXIT - DAY

MUSIC CONT.

The SUV rushes out SQUEALING in a tight turn, away from the wreckage in the background.

MUSIC ENDS

INT. RICHARD'S CAR - DAY

                    RICHARD
          (Mumbling) I'm not done
          fighting, you son of a bitch.

INT. SUV - DAY

DREAD drives. AHAB pulls out a burner phone, dials.

INT. SPEARING'S STUDY - DAY

ANGLE ON an old edition of *Frankenstein* on a mahogany desk. A burner phone beside the book BUZZES.

The manicured hand of WILLIAM SPEARING (We do NOT see his face) picks up the phone.

                    SPEARING (O.C.)
          Yes.

                    AHAB (O.S.)
          The problem is solved.

                    SPEARING (O.C.)
          You're sure he's dead?

                    AHAB (O.S.)
          Yes.

                    SPEARING (O.C.)
          Good.

EXT. SUV - DAY

The SUV rushes through an alley. AHAB's phone falls
in the gutter.

INT. STUDY - DAY

SPEARING's hand types a text: RICHARD IS DEAD.

INT. SCIENCE LAB - DAY

The pocket in DEBORAH NORWICH's lab coat BUZZES. With
her face lost in shadows, she pulls out a burner
phone, reads the text from SPEARING. She texts back:
THANK GOD.

NORWICH then drops the phone into an industrial
blender and fires it up.

INT. AMBULANCE MOVING - DAY

RICHARD is on a gurney. The bolt sticks out of his
neck.

                    RICHARD
               (Whispering) Vengeance is
               mine, thus saith the Lord. I
               will survive. I will exact
               revenge.

                    EMT
               Easy, dude. Easy. We're
               almost there.

                    RICHARD
               (Whispering) Vengeance is
               mine. I will survive.

INT. STUDY - DAY

ANGLE ON: SPEARING's HANDS place a leather box with a
painting of a camel and a desert village scene on its
lid onto the copy of *Frankenstein*.

SPEARING gently opens the box to reveal his heroin
stash.

INT. ER - DAY

RICHARD is on a table and surrounded by doctors and
nurses.

                    RICHARD
          (Faintly) I will survive. I
          will destroy them all. I.
          Will.

                    DOCTOR
          We're losing him!

                    RICHARD
          (Fading) Survive.

Heart monitor switches to a long TONE. Flat-line.

INT. STUDY - DAY

SPEARING's hands calmly cook heroin on a tiny brass
stove.

INT. ER - DAY

STAFF backing away from the table, pulling off gloves.

                    NURSE
          His driver's license says
          he's a donor.

                    DOCTOR
          Okay. Let's move him to an OR
          and begin the harvest.

INT. STUDY - DAY

CLOSE UP of SPEARING's hand eases a needle into a
plump vein, then draws back the plunger on the
syringe. Bright red blood swirls into the vial.

The manicured hand gracefully plunges the heroin and
blood into his arm. SPEARING gently draws the needle
from his arm.

INT. OR - DAY

A NURSE gently draws the bolt from RICHARD's neck.

                    RICHARD (V.O.)
          I will survive. I will exact
          revenge. I will destroy them
          all.

EXT. SKIES ABOVE LEXINGTON, KY - DAY

A medical helicopter approaches a hospital.

TITLE CARD: SAINT VINCENT'S HOSPITAL - LEXINGTON, KY.

INT. HOSPITAL HALLWAY - DAY

The STAFF quickly roll a bed down the hall. In the bed
is ETHAN BLAKE, a pudgy, ill, 40-something.

ETHAN is dark skinned with brown eyes, a Native
American.

BEVERLY BLAKE, ETHAN's white, blond wife rushes to his
bed.

                    BEVERLY
          Ethan, I'm sorry. I just got
          here. I came when they
          called.

                    ETHAN
          I know. It's botched already.
          The donor hospital forgot to
          call until the chopper was
          almost here. Just my luck.

                    BEVERLY
          It's okay, Ethan. It's gonna
          be OK.

                    ETHAN
          I guess so.

                    BEVERLY
          New Heart, New Start.
          Remember? We agreed on that.

                    ETHAN
          I'll try. For you.

                    NURSE
          This is as far as you can go,
          Mrs. Blake.

The bed CRASHES through a pair of doors.

                    BEVERLY
          I love you, Ethan.

                    ETHAN
          (calls back) Love you, Bev.

INT. OR - DAY

MUSIC by Beethoven plays in the operating theater.

ETHAN is anesthetized upon the table.

NURSE 2 lifts RICHARD's bagged heart out of a medical
cooler. She eases it from the bag into a bowl of
saline.

The heart has a faint glow, a blue aura.

DR. TANNER enters the OR in a special wheelchair. He
eases up to the table and pushes a button.

The wheelchair, a "standing wheelchair," reconfigures
itself into the standing position for DR. TANNER.

                    DR. TANNER
          Okay. Let's get this party
          started. (Beat) Where the
          hell is Dr. Young?

DR. YOUNG, who *is* young, stumbles through the door.

                    DR. YOUNG
          I'm here. I'm ...

DR. YOUNG crashes into an instrument table. CRASH!
CLATTER!

                    DR. TANNER
          Oh gawd. Somebody call the
          exterminators. We have an
          infestation of interns.

                    DR. YOUNG
          Sorry, Dr. Tanner.

                    DR. TANNER
          You're the one who signed up
          for a rotation with me.
          "Sorry" doesn't cut it. Just
          get over here without
          knocking Mr. Blake off the
          table.

                    DR. YOUNG
          Yes, sir.

                    DR. TANNER
          And somebody turn off that
          gawd-damned Beethoven. Mozart
          is the real master. (Beat)
          Scalpel!

INT. OR - LATER THAT DAY

Vivaldi MUSIC is playing.

ANGLE ON: Richard's heart in ETHAN'S chest cavity.
Dr. Tanner is finishing a suture on an artery.

                    DR. TANNER
          Okay, let's loosen the
          clamps. Get the de-fib
          paddles ready.

                    TECHNICIAN (O.C.)
          De-fib ready.

DR. TANNER loosens the clamps on the arteries, and the
heart pumps in a healthy rhythm.

                    DR. YOUNG
          What the ...?

                    DR. TANNER
          That's right. This heart
          wants to live so much all it
          needs is a little fresh
          blood. We don't even have to
          kick start it.

                    DR. YOUNG
          Amazing!

                    DR. TANNER
          Still want to shrink heads
          for a living, Dr. Young?
          Come on. Real men crack
          chests.

                              15

Dr. YOUNG stares on in awe.

                    DR. TANNER (CONT'D)
          Okay, back to work. I see a
          bleeder. Suction.

ANGLE ON a plain face in the OR door window, SISTER
RITA, a nun in full habit watches.

                    DR. TANNER (CONT'D)(O.C.)
          And turn on the machine that
          goes ping!

EVERYONE in the OR LAUGHS. SISTER RITA does not.

INT. CCU/ETHAN'S ROOM - EVENING

ETHAN is barely awake. BEVERLY fusses over her
husband.

                    BEVERLY
          I'm so glad it's over. Good
          to have you back where I can
          watch you. You know?

DR. TANNER wheels into the room in his special chair.
He looks at his iPad more than he does Ethan.

                    DR. TANNER
          Ah. Awake I see. Good.
          Ethan, I just wanted you to
          know the surgery went very
          well, and you that have an
          excellent, new heart. If you
          follow my orders, you should
          soon feel better than you
          have in years.

                    ETHAN
          (Raspy). Thanks Dr. Tanner.
          I already feel ... warmer.

                    DR. TANNER
          That's a good sign. It means
          your blood is circulating
          better. You'll start feeling
          post-op pain soon, so buzz
          the nurse when you do.

                    ETHAN
          (Drifting back to sleep) Did
          you give me a new soul, too?

ETHAN is asleep. BEVERLY looks at DR. TANNER who looks at his iPad and enters more data.

                    BEVERLY
          What an odd thing to say.

                    DR. TANNER
          I wouldn't worry about it.
          That's just his medications
          talking. (Beat) Let the
          nurses know if you need
          anything.

DR. TANNER wheels out of CCU.

INT. CCU/ETHAN'S ROOM - NIGHT

ETHAN is alone and asleep in his bed.

                    ETHAN
          (In his sleep) I will
          survive. I will destroy them
          all.

INT. CCU/ETHAN'S ROOM - DAY

ETHAN is sitting up slightly with a heart shaped pillow on his chest. He's still groggy.

SISTER RITA, in full habit, enters the room.

                    SISTER RITA
          Good morning, Mr. Blake. I'm
          Sister Rita. How are you
          feeling?

                    ETHAN
          Okay, I guess, all things
          considered.

                    SISTER RITA
          May I get you anything?

                    ETHAN
          Not that I can think of.
          Thanks.

                    SISTER RITA
          I'll check on you at least
          once a day. I can get you
          reading materials, snacks, or
          other things you might need.

                    ETHAN
          Thank you.

                    SISTER RITA
          I am also here for spiritual
          support, if you wish.

                    ETHAN
          Thanks. I doubt I'll need
          that.

                    SISTER RITA
          I understand.

SISTER RITA turns to leave.

                    ETHAN
          Wait. I'm not Catholic, or
          anything else really, but
          wasn't there a Saint Rita or
          something.

SISTER RITA looks back at ETHAN.

                    SISTER RITA
          Yes. I assumed her name when
          I took my vows.

                    ETHAN
          Was, I mean, is she a patron
          or whatever?

                    SISTER RITA
          Rita is the patron saint of
          impossibilities.

SISTER RITA walks out.

INT. VARIOUS HOSPITAL SHOTS/MONTAGE

CUE MUSIC: "Making a Noise," by Robbie Robertson

Slow paced montage of ETHAN'S recovery.

- ETHAN walking with help.

- BEVERLY fussing over ETHAN.

- ETHAN turning his nose up at the hospital food.

- ETHAN in physical therapy.

- ETHAN eating better.

- ETHAN studying the scar on his chest in a mirror.

- ETHAN studying an attractive nurse's figure.

- ETHAN on a stationary bike.

INT. HOSPITAL HALLWAY - DAY

MUSIC CONT.

ETHAN, in bathrobe, walks down the hall and spies something on a housekeeping buggy.

ANGLE ON: A pack of Camel cigarettes and lighter on top of the buggy.

ETHAN looks around to see if anyone is watching then slips the pack and lighter into his robe pocket.

INT. HOSPITAL ROOM - DAY

MUSIC CONT.

Shot of bathroom door. A smoke detector goes off. A piercing ALARM screams out.

A NURSE opens the door. ETHAN is inside, sitting, and trying to put out a cigarette while fanning smoke around.

> NURSE 3
> Smokin' in the boy's room are
> we, Mr. Blake?

MUSIC ENDS

INT. HOSPITAL ROOM - DAY

ETHAN is sitting up in bed, eating and half-watching
the TV news.

> NEWS ANCHOR
> A well-known drug kingpin was
> killed in Columbus, Ohio
> today, with a, get this, a
> crossbow. The arrow, or bolt
> as experts call it, went
> through his head execution
> style. Authorities have no
> real leads in the case, but
> this is the fourth such
> killing in recent weeks.
> Three weeks ago, an FBI agent
> and an informant were killed
> with a crossbow in a
> Washington, DC parking
> garage. Last week, another
> top drug dealer, this time in
> Detroit, was similarly
> executed. The FBI is
> investigating. (Beat) In
> other news tonight ....

DR. YOUNG enters the room with an iPad in his hand.

> DR. YOUNG
> Mr. Blake? Hi. I'm Doctor
> Michael Young. How are you
> today?

ETHAN hits the remote and turns off the TV.

> ETHAN
> I'm not living the dream, but
> I'm not living the nightmare
> either.

> DR. YOUNG
> (Chuckling) Good to hear. May
> I sit down?

> ETHAN
> Sure.

DR. YOUNG pulls up a chair and sits.

> DR. YOUNG
> So. I'm an intern here. I
> plan to specialize in
> psychiatry, but I'm doing a

cardiac rotation now. I
watched your transplant the
other day.

                    ETHAN
You think I need a
psychiatrist?

                    DR. YOUNG
No, not at all. It's just
that many people go through
depression after major
surgery. I plan to do
research in that area. I want
to see what they go through
physically as well as
mentally. It gives me
context.

                    ETHAN
Sure the "context" doesn't
have to do with me trying to
smoke a cigarette yesterday?

                    DR. YOUNG
No. I was planning to visit
you before that. But just
what was that about anyway?

                    ETHAN
I don't know. Something just
possessed me. Like a memory I
don't really have. You know?

                    DR. YOUNG
Not really, no.

                    ETHAN
I saw the pack and just
suddenly had to have one.

                    DR. YOUNG
According to your transplant
registry application, you
never smoked before. Is that
true?

                    ETHAN
I swear. That's the truth.

                    DR. YOUNG
Well, make sure that was not
only your first cigarette,
but also your last.

                    ETHAN
          Yeah. Dr. Tanner jumped all
          over me last night.

                    DR. YOUNG
          I can imagine. He's tough.

                    ETHAN
          He's a cold fish.

                    DR. YOUNG
          How do you mean?

                    ETHAN
          He cares more about hearts
          and arteries than about the
          people. (Beat) You won't tell
          him I said that, will you?

                    DR. YOUNG (chuckling)
          Your secret is safe.

DR. YOUNG swipes his iPad..

                    DR. YOUNG (CONT'D)
          I have a few notes here about
          your treatment. This is for
          my research. Mind if I ask
          you a few questions?

                    ETHAN
          Admit it. You really are
          going to psycho-analyze me,
          aren't you?

                    DR. YOUNG
          No, Mr. Blake. I just want to
          gather information for future
          reference. For example. I
          notice you've checked both
          the Caucasian and Native
          American boxes on the
          hospital forms. So I assume
          you're part-Indian then?

                    ETHAN
          No. I'm part white.

                    DR. YOUNG
          Oh, um, OK, what tribe are
          you from then?

                    ETHAN
          Cherokee.

                    DR. YOUNG
          Did you grow up on a
          reservation?

                    ETHAN
          No. My ancestors were on the
          Trail of Tears. When they
          walked through Kentucky, they
          got tired of that shit and
          escaped one night. They wound
          up in a town just south of
          here, blended in, and bought
          a farm. That's where I live
          now. Four generations.

                    DR. YOUNG
          Wow.

                    ETHAN
          And I'll be the last one
          there.

                    DR. YOUNG
          Why?

                    ETHAN
          I have a mighty fine gun, Dr.
          Young, but it fires blanks.

                    DR. YOUNG
          (Puzzled) Meaning? Oh I got
          you. Well. I'm, I'm sorry.
          But you could always adopt a
          baby.

                    ETHAN
          Bev and I used to talk about
          that, but now, the medical
          bills ... I'll be paying for
          this heart for the rest of my
          life.

                    DR. YOUNG
          Yes, I see. (Beat) I notice
          you said "this heart" instead
          of "my heart." How does it
          feel to have had a
          transplant?

                    ETHAN
          What you really want to know
          is: What's it like to have
          another man's heart in my
          chest.

                       23

                    DR. YOUNG
Well. Yes.

                    ETHAN
It's kinda weird. Someone had
to die. And I had nothing to
do with that, but now I go on
living with his misfortune. A
part of him goes where I go.

                    DR. YOUNG
Does that bother you?

                    ETHAN
You have to understand.
Everyone says to me, "Hey,
Ethan, you got a new heart!"
Except I don't. It's like
buying a car at the used car
lot. It's new to me; that's
all.

                    DR. YOUNG
You sound bitter about the
whole thing, Mr. Blake. About
life in general, I mean.

                    ETHAN
No. I just like to be left
alone. I'm an independent man
who has been poked and
prodded and handled. I'm
grateful for the second
chance at life, I guess. But
I am tired of waiting for it
to start.

                    DR. YOUNG
In that case, I have good
news for you, Mr. Blake.
You're going home tomorrow.

                    ETHAN
Whew. 'Bout time.

                    DR. YOUNG
There is one condition.

                    ETHAN
A catch you mean.

                    DR. YOUNG
You'll have a session with me
every time you come back for

a checkup with Dr. Tanner.

                    ETHAN
          (Pauses) Anything to get out
          of this dump.

EXT. HOSPITAL ENTRANCE - EVENING

BEVERLY approaches the entrance but is stopped by
SISTER RITA.

                    SISTER RITA
          Mrs. Blake.

                    BEVERLY
          Yes?

                    SISTER RITA
          I'm Sister Rita. I have
          visited with Mr. Blake a few
          times.

                    BEVERLY
          Well. Thank you.

                    SISTER RITA
          Your husband gets to go home
          tomorrow.

                    BEVERLY
          Oh good. I knew it was about
          time.

                    SISTER RITA
          I should tell you something
          else.

                    BEVERLY
          What's that?

                    SISTER RITA
          Mr. Blake has been given a
          great gift. I hope he is
          prepared for it.

                    BEVERLY
          He seems to be doing well -
          unless there's something they
          haven't told me. Is there?

                    SISTER RITA
          Years ago I had a vision.
          Mr. Blake was in it. Of
          that, I am certain. I also
          saw planets, violence, and
          the birth of a new epoch. I
          think he plays a crucial role
          in these things.

                    BEVERLY
          O. K. then. I'm not sure ...

                    SISTER RITA
          (Interrupting) Are you a
          woman of faith, Mrs. Blake?

                    BEVERLY
          Yes. I was raised Methodist.
          I still pray fairly often.
          I've prayed a lot for Ethan.

                    SISTER RITA
          Good. Continue to pray for
          him. And for yourself. There
          will be many difficulties,
          but in the end, when I see
          you again, it will be
          wonderful.

SISTER RITA rushes off, disappears in a crowd.

                    BEVERLY
          How bizarre.

INT.   HOSPITAL ROOM - NIGHT

ETHAN is asleep, but restless. He dreams.

DREAM SCENE: ETHAN is in RICHARD'S seat in RICHARD'S
car. He sees the scene from RICHARD'S point of view as
the car lurches forward, causing DREADS and AHAB to
scatter. The car crashes into STANLEY and off the top
of the parking garage. ETHAN SCREAMS as they plummet
to the street below. After they crash into the street.

ETHAN wakes up SCREAMING in his hospital room.

INT.   SCIENCE LAB - NIGHT

NASIM, a technician and Persian woman, is glued to
computer screens full of numbers. The room is dark.

NORWICH approaches NASIM, her face barely visible in
the glow from the computer screens.

                    NORWICH
          What did you find, Nasim?

                    NASIM
          I found this tiny object out
          past Mars and Saturn, just
          where you said it would be,
          Professor Norwich.

                    NORWICH
          So I see. Good work.

                    NASIM
          How did you know where to
          look? It's so small.

                    NORWICH
          Just a hunch. (Beat). I want
          you to track it, Nasim. I
          want you to follow its every
          move. And Nasim?

                    NASIM
          Yes, Professor Norwich?

                    NORWICH
          This stays between you and me
          for now - until we know what
          it is.

                    NASIM (smiling)
          Of course.

EXT. COUNTRY ROAD - DAY

BEVERLY is driving a car. ETHAN is in the passenger
seat.

The car pulls onto a long dirt driveway that leads to
a small farm.

INT. FARMHOUSE ENTRYWAY - DAY

The door opens, and ETHAN walks in. BEVERLY follows.

>   BEVERLY
>   Welcome home to you and your
>   new heart.

>   ETHAN
>   It feels like it's been years
>   instead of a few lonely
>   weeks.

>   BEVERLY
>   Lonely? I've been with you
>   everyday, maybe not as
>   much...

>   ETHAN
>   (Interrupting) I mean (beat),
>   I'm only lonely when I don't
>   get to be alone with you.

>   BEVERLY
>   Oh Ethan, that's so sweet.
>   And a good save.

BEVERLY and ETHAN kiss, become passionate.

>   BEVERLY (CONT)
>   What did Dr. Tanner say about
>   extracurricular activities?

>   ETHAN
>   That you should be on top.

BEVERLY and ETHAN head up stairs laughing.

[SCREENBOOK NOTE: Though it is absolutely unnecessary
to the film and would get cut in editing (we hope),
feel free to imagine the homecoming sex scene of a
heart transplant patient here - set to the song "Total
Eclipse of the Heart" by Bonnie Tyler. You're
welcome.]

INT. FARM HOUSE KITCHEN - MORNING.

BEVERLY and ETHAN are eating breakfast.

>   BEVERLY
>   I'm sorry I have to teach
>   today. Doesn't seem fair on

your first full day back
home.

              ETHAN
It's okay. You've already
missed too much.

              BEVERLY
Do you have any plans for
today?

              ETHAN
I thought I'd visit with
Sophia.

              BEVERLY
I figured. Just don't over
do.

              ETHAN
I won't. (Beat) I thought I'd
call the store. See if I
still have a job.

              BEVERLY
(Sighs). I already know the
answer to that, dear heart.

              ETHAN
(Suspiciously) And?

              BEVERLY
The store is closing, Ethan.
I saw Mr. Flint last week.
He's going out of business.
I'm sorry.

              ETHAN
Nobody needs carpet anymore?

              BEVERLY
They go to the big chain
stores when they do. Most
people get that laminate wood
stuff. Everything changes.

              ETHAN
Damn.

              BEVERLY
I know, but, I was thinking …
You're such a good writer.
You have such a tremendous
imagination and all, why

don't you try writing again?
Write your novel.

                    ETHAN
          I don't know, Bev. I mean...

                    BEVERLY
          You could clean out the junk
          room and turn it into a
          study.

                    ETHAN
          You mean the future nursery.

                    BEVERLY
          We know that's out of the
          question for now, so...

BEV stands, rinses off a plate in the
sink, glances out the window.

                    ETHAN
          It's my fault, I know, so
          using the room for a writer's
          cave -- I can't do that.
          That'd just suck, and...

                    BEVERLY
          (Interrupting) Okay, okay. So
          forget that. But with the
          laptop, you can write
          anywhere in the house -- even
          the barn.

                    ETHAN
          I'll think about it.

BEV turns back to Ethan, forces herself
to smile.

                    BEVERLY
          New Heart, New Start!

                    ETHAN
          (Chuckling) I'll think about
          it.

BEVERLY gathers her things, kisses ETHAN, and rushes
for the back door.

                    BEVERLY (CONT'D)
          Enjoy your day with Sophia.
          Love you, Bye.

BEVERLY closes the door.

                    ETHAN
          Bye.

EXT. FARM/BARN - DAY

ETHAN leads SOPHIA, a brown, black, and white horse,
out into the farmyard and sunshine.

ETHAN and SOPHIA stop under a shade tree. He gives
her a carrot and brushes her.

                    ETHAN
          Did you miss me, Sophia? Has
          Uncle John been good to you?
          (Pause) A lot's happened
          since I last saw you, girl.
          I should have died, my old
          ticker was so bad. But those
          doctors saved my life. I
          still don't know if that's a
          good thing or a bad thing. I
          guess we'll just have to wait
          and see. Huh?

INT. BARN - DAY

ETHAN carefully "tucks" SOPHIA into her stall with
fresh straw, pats her on the snout with a lingering
glance.

ETHAN walks toward the barn doors. He "hears"
RICHARD'S disembodied voice.

                    RICHARD (O.C.)
          Ethan?

ETHAN looks around for the source of this voice.

                    RICHARD (CONT'D) (O.C.)
          Ethan.

                    ETHAN
          Who's there?

                    RICHARD (O.C.)
          You won't be able to see me,
          I'm afraid.

                          31

                    ETHAN
          Who are you? Is that you
          Uncle John? Come out here.
          Kind of a mean joke to play!

                    RICHARD (O.C.)
          I'm not your Uncle John. My
          name is Richard, and I'm --
          I'm inside you.

                    ETHAN
          (Still looking around) What?

                    RICHARD (O.C.)
          I am the owner of your new
          heart. *Was* the owner.

                    ETHAN
          WHAT!?

                    RICHARD (O.C.)
          I know this is hard to
          believe, but I have survived
          with the heart. My soul or
          spirit or whatever, it's now
          inside of you.

                    ETHAN
          I'm going fucking crazy.

                    RICHARD (O.C.)
          No. You're not crazy.

ETHAN steps out of the barn.

EXT. BARNYARD - DAY

ETHAN grabs his head and walks faster.

                    ETHAN
          Oh my God. Oh my God. They're
          gonna lock me in the loony
          bin.

                    RICHARD (O.C.)
          Take it easy, man. You're
          gonna be OK. Trust me.

                    ETHAN
          What am I going to do? God
          help me. Please help me, God.

                    RICHARD (O.C.)
          Calm down, Ethan. Steady
          yourself, man.

                    ETHAN
          This can't be happening. I'm
          hearing things.

                    RICHARD (O.C.)
          Just calm down. I can prove I
          exist.

                    ETHAN
          Over the rainbow, I'm crazy.
          Oh God help me.

                    RICHARD (O.C.)
          You're fine, Ethan. I can
          prove this is real.

          ETHAN stops walking. Pauses a moment, breathing hard,
          about to hyperventilate. ETHAN addresses the voice
          for the first time.

                    ETHAN
          How -- how would you do that?

                    RICHARD (O.C.)
          We need to get to a computer.

                    ETHAN
          This is Batman & Joker crazy.
          This is headless chickens
          crazy.

                    RICHARD (O.C.)
          (Interrupting) I can prove I
          exist. You can read my
          obituary on-line.

                    ETHAN
          Great. The little voice is
          giving me orders. Oh God,
          this can't be happening! No.
          No.

                    RICHARD (O.C.)
          At least I can prove I exist,
          and you will know you are not
          crazy.

          ETHAN clams himself a little, slows his
          breath, steadies his hands a bit.

                    ETHAN
          OK, OK. Let's say you can
          prove this, this shit is --
          real. What then?

                    RICHARD (O.C.)
          Then we've got work to do.

INT.   FARMHOUSE - DAY

ETHAN CLICKS away at a computer.

                    RICHARD (O.C.)
          My name is Richard Hamlin. I
          was born on May 1, 1988. I
          did a stint in the Army, in
          Iraq. I was in Special Ops.
          Then I joined the FBI. I grew
          up in Baltimore, so look for
          my obituary in *The Sun*. My
          father, Luke, is my sole
          survivor.

A photo of RICHARD in full dress uniform flashes up on
the screen.

                    ETHAN (To himself)
          You did exist.

                    RICHARD (O.C.)
          I *do* exist. (Beat) I was
          killed by a drug lord in a
          parking garage in Washington,
          DC. Google that.

ETHAN types more on the computer. A photo of Richard's
smashed car fills the screen.

                    ETHAN
          Oh my God. They did that to
          you?

                    RICHARD (O.C.)
          Yes.

                    ETHAN (V.O.)
          I remember this, the car
          crashing off a building. I
          thought it was a nightmare,
          but it was a memory, your
          memory.

                    RICHARD (O.C.)
          Yes.

                    ETHAN (V.O.)
          Then I'm not crazy.

                    RICHARD (O.C.)
          You're not crazy.

                    ETHAN (V.O.)
          Then you see what I see, hear
          what I hear?

                    RICHARD (O.C.)
          Yes. I can.

                    ETHAN (Out loud)
          You can read my thoughts?

                    RICHARD (O.C.)
          Yes.

ETHAN contemplates this a moment, then SCREAMS.

FADE TO BLACK

INT. EXAM ROOM - DAY

ETHAN sits on the exam table. DR. YOUNG enters the
room.

                    DR. YOUNG
          Hello, Ethan. To what do I
          owe this surprise?

                    ETHAN
          I --I have a man inside of
          me.

                    DR. YOUNG
          (Chuckles a bit) What, uh,
          what did you just say?

                    ETHAN
          I have a man living inside of
          me. He talks to me.

                    RICHARD (O.C.)[1]
          Told you he wouldn't believe
          you.

                    DR. YOUNG
          You mean you hear voices?

                    ETHAN
          Not voices. A voice. It's the
          man who had this heart that
          you people shoved into my
          chest!

     DR. YOUNG, the shrink-in-training, sees a great case.

                    DR. YOUNG
          How long has this been
          happening?

                    ETHAN
          It started this morning.
          You've got to help me, Dr.
          Young. You've got to help me
          get rid of Richard.

                    DR. YOUNG
          Richard?

                    ETHAN
          That's his name. He was an
          FBI agent, killed by drug
          dealers.

                    DR. YOUNG
          Ethan. You know that's not
          possible.

                    ETHAN
          But I read his obituary.

                    DR. YOUNG
          Ah. I see what's happened.
          You got curious about your
          donor -- that's normal, and
          you looked at obits of people
          who died on the date you got

_____

     [1]For the rest of the story/film, "RICHARD (O.C.)"
means only Ethan can hear him. RICHARD's "voice" is
in Ethan's "mind."

your heart. You found one and your imagination got the best of you.

                    ETHAN
Wait. Remember how I smoked a Camel cigarette here in the hospital. Richard says that's his brand.

                    DR. YOUNG
(Chuckling) That's just an urban myth. Guy gets out of the hospital after a liver transplant and makes his wife stop at Wendy's on the way home. He eats burgers like they're going to stop making them. Doctor checks it out, and sure enough, that was the donor's favorite food. But that's all it is, Ethan, a myth.

                    ETHAN
You think I'm crazy.

                    DR. YOUNG
"Crazy" is such a vague term. I think you're having trouble with the idea that someone else's heart is inside your body.

                    RICHARD (O.C.)
He thinks you have toys in your attic.

                    ETHAN
Listen, Doctor Young. I'm not crazy.

                    DR. YOUNG
Ethan. Ethan. Get a grip.

                    RICHARD (O.C.)
Tell him we want to make a deal.

                    ETHAN
Richard wants to make a deal with you.

                    DR. YOUNG

You mean you can hear him
now?

                    ETHAN
Of course.

                    DR. YOUNG
OK. I'll play along. What
kind of deal does "Richard"
want to make?

                    RICHARD (O.C.)
Order a PET scan.

                    ETHAN
He wants you to do a PET
scan.

                    DR. YOUNG
A PET? Do you have any idea
what that costs?

                    ETHAN
Hell. I don't even know what
it is.

                    DR. YOUNG
Then why do you want one?

                    ETHAN
I don't. Richard does.

                    DR. YOUNG
(Sighs) And why does
"Richard" want it?

                    RICHARD (O.C.)
A PET will show our brain
activity and open his mind.

                    ETHAN
He says it'll show you our
brain activity and open your
mind.

                    DR. YOUNG
And what else does Richard
say?

Pause.

                    ETHAN
          He says you're the biggest
          asshole he's seen since
          coming to Lexington.

INT. PET SCAN ROOM - DAY

MUSIC for this scene: Pink Floyd's "Brain Damage".

The PET TECH and DR. YOUNG sit in the control room.
Through a window we see ETHAN in the PET machine.

                    DR. YOUNG (INTO INTERCOM MIC)
          OK, Ethan. We're starting.

Images of Ethan's brain flicker onto the TECH's
computer screen. The brain is mostly purple and blue.

                    PET TECH
          (To Dr. Young) It's normal.
          What are you looking for?

                    DR. YOUNG
          (To PET TECH) Honestly? No
          Idea. (To Ethan via intercom)
          I'm sorry ETHAN, but there's
          nothing abnormal here.

                    ETHAN
          Richard says he's going to
          plug into my wiring now,
          whatever that means.

The PET TECH peers out at ETHAN to see who else is
there. He shakes his head when he sees no one but
Ethan and looks at the computer screen again.

Two regions of ETHAN'S frontal lobe turn yellow then
red. These spread until the whole brain is dark
yellow and red.

                    DR. YOUNG
          (To PET TECH) You ever seen
          anything like this before?

                    PET TECH
          Not even close for someone
          just layin' there. His brain
          looks like he's juggling
          chainsaws while walking a
          tightrope.

                         39

Small red and white spots begin popping on and off in
rapid succession.

                    PET TECH (CONT'D)
          His brain is a freaking
          Christmas tree.

                    DR. YOUNG
          What in God's name ... (To
          Ethan via Intercom) OK,
          Ethan. My mind is definitely
          open.

END MUSIC

INT. SCIENCE LAB - NIGHT

NASIM THE LAB TECH is studying her computer screens
full of numbers. She is blurry eyed and slightly
disheveled.

PROF. NORWICH walks in, properly pressed.

                    NORWICH
          What do you see, Nasim?

                    NASIM
          The object is definitely out
          there, as you predicted.

                    NORWICH
          Theorized.

                    NASIM
          Theorized. And when it passes
          Mars, there's a good chance
          it will swing around and head
          toward earth, depending on
          its density.

                    NORWICH
          Good. Anything else?

                    NASIM
          There's a slight chance we
          could pick it up with the
          Hubble telescope in a week or
          two.

                    NORWICH
          No. I'm not ready to tell the
          others about it just yet.

                    NASIM
          Whatever. It's your rock to
          rock.

                    NORWICH
          That's just the thing, Nasim.
          It's not a rock.

INT. FARMHOUSE KITCHEN - NIGHT

An old radio plays "Every Breath You Take" by The
Police.

ETHAN, in pajamas, stands at the stove frying bologna.

BEVERLY enters the kitchen in a nightgown.

                    BEVERLY
          Ethan, it's 2 in the morning.
          What in Job's name are you
          doing?

                    ETHAN
          Making a midnight snack.

                    BEVERLY
          (Sighs) What's wrong?

                    ETHAN
          Nothing. Why?

                    BEVERLY
          Fried bologna is your comfort
          food.

                    ETHAN
          Nothing's wrong. I just
          wanted it.

                    BEVERLY
          Come on. Spill it.
          Something's bothering you.

                    ETHAN
          Maybe the transplant myths
          are true. Maybe my new heart
          likes midnight snacks.

                    BEVERLY
          I think you're lying.

                    ETHAN
          I think my heart's donor had
          a wife who fixed him a
          bologna sandwich whenever he
          wanted one.

                    BEVERLY
          You know what? Fine. Play
          stoic Indian if you want. I
          gotta teach in the morning.

BEVERLY turns and exits the kitchen.

ETHAN plops a piece of bologna on a slice of toast,
covers it with mustard, then covers it with another
slice of toast.

                    ETHAN
          (To himself) I wouldn't even
          know what to tell you, Bev.
          I don't think you'd like
          Richard one bit.

ETHAN bites into his sandwich.

MUSIC ENDS.

INT. DR. TANNER'S OFFICE - DAY

DR. TANNER works at his desk. There's a KNOCK at his
door.

                    DR. TANNER
          What!

DR. YOUNG walks in.

                    DR. TANNER (CONT'D)
          What do you want, Young?

                    DR. YOUNG
          It's Mr. Blake, the heart
          transplant.

                    DR. TANNER
          What about him?

                    DR. YOUNG
          Well, he claims to hear the
          voice of the donor in his
          head.

                         DR. TANNER
                    Isn't psychosis your
                    department?

                         DR. YOUNG
                    Yes, but I ran these tests
                    yesterday, and I did research
                    all night and ...

DR. YOUNG hands DR. TANNER papers and charts. DR.
TANNER takes a rudimentary peek at them.

                         DR. TANNER
                    Let me get this straight: You
                    think there really is someone
                    inside Mr. Blake?

                         DR. YOUNG
                    Well. Yes.

                         DR. TANNER
                    Then you belong on the psyche
                    ward with him.

                         DR. YOUNG
                    Is it really out of the realm
                    of possibility?

The faint sound of SIRENS seeps into the room.

                         DR. TANNER
                    I knew you were a flake, but
                    this beats everything.

TANNER begins moving his wheelchair to the door.

                         DR. TANNER (CONT'D)
                    Follow me. We have real work
                    to do.

                         DR. YOUNG
                    Pardon?

                         DR. TANNER
                    If you had been paying
                    attention, you'd know the ER
                    is in CODE RED. A pile-up on
                    I-64. All hands on deck.

INT. HOSPITAL HALLWAY - DAY

DR. TANNER wheels out of his office. DR. YOUNG
follows. THEY head for the ER in a busy hallway.

DR. TANNER hits the up button on his chair and slowly "stands" up even as the chair rolls forward.

                    DR. YOUNG
          But the PET scan ...

                    DR. TANNER
          (Interrupting). It is a
          biological impossibility.
          You're on a ghost hunt.

DR. TANNER is now taller than DR. YOUNG.

                    DR. YOUNG
          The theory that the mind is
          merely part of the body is
          relatively new. Plato
          believed in a separate soul.
          Descartes argued the mind
          existed separately ...

                    DR. TANNER
          (Interrupting) Descartes was
          rejected in favor of
          materialism years ago.

                    DR. YOUNG
          Cultures throughout the world
          believe the soul and mind
          rest with the heart.
          Cannibals eat the heart to
          get ...

THEY enter the chaos of the ER.

                    DR. TANNER
          (Interrupting) You're
          grasping at straws with
          sophomoric philosophy. Do you
          have any real proof?

THEY pause a moment. DR. YOUNG is defeated.

                    DR. TANNER (CONT'D)
          You mean you're wasting my
          time with a few odd scans and
          feather-weight research. I
          should dismiss you from your
          residency.

DR. TANNER rolls into an open ER AREA with several injured victims already piling up. DR. YOUNG follows. NURSES and DOCTORS are rushing about. Patients are MOANING.

DR. TANNER rolls up to a table with a mess of a little
girl on it -- blood everywhere, a piece of metal
sticks out of her chest. He looks over her body, into
her eyes. Her skin is ashen, eyes wide open. She's
already dead.

SISTER RITA, in habit, is at the head. She has a
latex-covered hand pressed against the child's temple.

                    DR. TANNER
          Sister, what is this you're
          doing?

                    SISTER RITA
          (With no emotion) An EMT was
          doing this. She asked me to
          take over.

DR. TANNER looks more closely, then tugs at SISTER
RITA'S hand for a better look.

DR. YOUNG peers in as well.

                    SISTER RITA (CONT'D)
          I'm holding the bone and
          brain in place.

                    DR. TANNER
          I see. (Beat) Sister, you may
          let go now. This child is
          already gone.

                    SISTER RITA
          Doctor?

                    DR. TANNER
          She's bled out. No oxygen to
          the brain in at least a half
          hour. She only needs for me
          to declare her dead. (Beat)
          Go help the living, Sister.

SISTER RITA retreats. The skull and brain slop onto
the table. DR. YOUNG nearly throws up.

DR. TANNER points at the wrecked brain matter.

                    DR. TANNER (CONT'D)
          There, Dr. Young, is the seat
          of the soul, the mind, the
          identity of this child. But
          those things are gone now.
          The human mind is nothing but
          the activity of the brain.

                    This brain's dead, so this
                    child no longer exists.
                    Understand?

DR. YOUNG nods his head "yes."

DR. TANNER picks up a chart and pulls out a pen.

                         DR. TANNER (CONT'D)
                    Time of death: 3:57. (BEAT)
                    Quit screwing around, Doctor
                    Young. Get new DNA samples
                    from several places in Mr.
                    Blake's body. Compare them to
                    the heart's. When they don't
                    match, you'll see how idiotic
                    your theory is.

                         DR. YOUNG
                    I- I hadn't thought of that.

                         DR. TANNER
                    Welcome to your residency,
                    Doctor. (Beat). Now practice
                    your suturing skills. God
                    knows there are plenty of
                    wounds here today. Go save a
                    life.

INT. FARMHOUSE - DAY

ETHAN stares at his computer screen. All he has
written is: THEN THE SOON-TO-BE-FAMOUS AUTHOR DIED OF
BOREDOM.

                         RICHARD (O.C.)
                    You know, Bev's not going to
                    think much of that first
                    line.

                         ETHAN
                    Shut up.

                         RICHARD (O.C.)
                    Really think you got what it
                    takes to be a writer?

                         ETHAN
                    Oh great. Another artistic
                    vampire in my head.

                    RICHARD (O.C.)
               Just saying.

ETHAN picks up a new pack of regular Camel cigarettes,
studies the front.

ANGLE ON: Pack, the words "Turkish and Domestic
blend."

ETHAN turns the pack over: Yellow/gold drawing of
minarets, palm trees.

                    ETHAN
               If I smoke a couple, will you
               leave me alone awhile?

                    RICHARD (O.C.)
               Now we're talking.

ETHAN opens the package, pulls out a cigarette and
lights up. He savors the taste a moment.

ETHAN begins CLICKING at the keyboard. He deletes what
he has already written.

ETHAN types: THE SURREAL JOURNAL OF ETHAN BLAKE

INT. SPEARING'S STUDY - NIGHT

ANGLE ON: An iPhone sits on the illustration of
Sherlock Holmes on a first edition copy of a *The
Seven-Per-Cent Solution: Being a Reprint from the
Reminiscences of John H. Watson, M.D.*

The phone RINGS with the name "KAREN" on the screen.

SPEARING answers. We only see his mouth and hands.

                    SPEARING
               Hello, Karen. What a long
               time it has been.

                    KAREN (O.S.)
               You had him killed, didn't
               you?

                    SPEARING
               Right to the point as always.
               Whom do you think I had --
               removed?

                    KAREN (O.S.)
          You know who, you bastard.
          Richard.

                    SPEARING
          No. I had nothing to do with
          that. Richard went in half-
          cocked as he always did. I
          tried to warn him. You *knew* -
          Richard better than I. You
          may well imagine.

                    KAREN (O.S.)
          You set him up. I'll prove
          it.

                    SPEARING
          Well, you always were my best
          -- agent. I'm sure you'll
          find the truth soon enough.
          (Beat). I miss you, Karen.

                    KAREN (O.S.)
          Don't even ...

                    SPEARING
          Everything is so personal
          with you.

                    KAREN (O.S.)
          You're chasing the dragon
          again, aren't you?

SPEARING'S fingers drum the top of his heroin kit.

                    SPEARING
          Of course not.

                    KAREN (O.S.)
          Or is it chasing the Camel
          now? You and Ahab buddies?

                    SPEARING
          No, my love. But I'm glad you
          worry over my health so.

                    KAREN (O.S.)
          I'll personally kill you if I
          find you set him up. That's
          your warning, Spearing, which
          is more than you gave
          Richard.

The line goes silent.

INT. DR. TANNER'S OFFICE - DAY

DR. TANNER sits at his desk. ETHAN sits across from
him. DR. YOUNG stands in a corner, arms crossed.

> DR. TANNER
> Here it is, Ethan. By
> comparing the DNA from
> various parts of your body,
> we were able to determine if
> something, or someone, were
> indeed spreading in your body
> from the harvested heart. An
> anomaly I could never have
> imagined possible.

> ETHAN
> And?

> DR. TANNER
> And, yes. I'm still trying to
> absorb this myself, but yes,
> something is happening to
> you, a side effect of sorts.

> ETHAN
> Then Richard exists?

> DR. TANNER
> It would appear some
> manifestation of the donor, a
> man named Richard Hamlin,
> exists within you.

> ETHAN
> Then I'm not crazy?

> DR. TANNER
> No.

PAUSE as ETHAN soaks in this revelation.

> ETHAN
> So how do we end this
> nightmare?

> DR. YOUNG
> (Clears throat) I'm afraid
> this is worse than you
> realize.

> ETHAN
> How?

                    DR. YOUNG
Richard appears to be doing
this on purpose.

                    ETHAN
What?

                    DR. YOUNG
Richard is wiring himself
into your brain and nervous
system. Your brain is doing
things at his direction, as
in the PET scans. Some how
the nerves from the heart are
branching into other parts of
your body.

                    DR. TANNER
The same way stroke patients
relearn language and speech.

                    DR. YOUNG
Some people believe our DNA
records everything that
happens in our lives.

                    DR. TANNER
It's called genetic memories.

                    DR. YOUNG
Right. Genetic memories could
explain Richard's presence in
your mind.

                    ETHAN
Meaning?

                    DR. YOUNG
Richard's DNA is now in the
bone marrow of your right
arm. Your body has over one
hundred trillion blood cells.
Three billion are replaced
every *second*. In this way,
Richard's DNA is spreading to
every part of your body.
This is a bit like stem cell
therapy.

                    DR. TANNER
To be blunt, Ethan, Richard
is intentionally weaving his
DNA and nervous system into
yours.

                    ETHAN
          Meaning?

                    DR. YOUNG
          Richard is taking over your
          body, your brain - and your
          mind.

FADE TO BLACK

INT. OLD TRUCK - MOVING - EVENING

ETHAN drives erratically on rural highways.

                    RICHARD (O.C.)
          What are you doing, Ethan?

                    ETHAN
          Driving.

                    RICHARD (O.C.)
          Where to?

                    ETHAN
          You'll see.

EXT. JESSE STUART BRIDGE - EVENING

ETHAN's TRUCK stops halfway across the large but
isolated bridge high above the Ohio River. [This is an
actual place and bridge.]

INT. TRUCK - STOPPED - EVENING

                    RICHARD (O.C.)
          Ethan?

ETHAN shuts off the engine and crawls out.

                    ETHAN
          I think you know.

EXT. JESSE STUART BRIDGE - EVENING

ETHAN climbs onto the wall on the side of the bridge.

ETHAN lifts his right foot for a last step.

>   RICHARD (O.C.)
>   Wimp.

ETHAN freezes.

>   RICHARD (O.C.)(CONT'D)
>   You're just another pussy
>   taking the easy road out of
>   town.

>   ETHAN
>   Your reverse psycho-shit
>   won't work on me.

>   RICHARD (O.C.)
>   So get it over with then.
>   Take a leap.

>   ETHAN
>   I intend to -- in peace.

>   RICHARD (O.C.)
>   I just have one question.
>   Consider it a dying man's
>   request.

ETHAN puts his foot back down.

>   ETHAN
>   What?

>   RICHARD (O.C.)
>   Why did you change your mind?

>   ETHAN
>   About what?

>   RICHARD (O.C.)
>   This. About staying alive.
>   You've made this choice
>   before. Life or death. I
>   found it among your recent
>   memories.

>   ETHAN
>   What?

>   RICHARD (O.C.)

A few weeks before you got me, you were clinically dead. You saw the bright light of eternity pierce the darkness of this world. You saw the very edge of paradise. You saw your parents waiting for you on the other side. Just a few steps and you would have left this pathetic world of pain and suffering behind you. But you didn't. You picked life instead. (Pause) Why did you make that choice, Ethan? Why return to this hell?

                    ETHAN
I don't know. Fear maybe.

                    RICHARD (O.C.)
No. It wasn't fear. You picked life because your life sucked. You wanted to try again. When God said "Game Over," You pressed the restart button.

                    ETHAN
Yeah. So?

                    RICHARD (O.C.)
You wanted a second chance to have an adventure. You wanted to really live a life, not just go through the motions.

                    ETHAN
Yes. But you weren't part of the deal. Now you've robbed me of that chance.

                    RICHARD (O.C.)
Have I? What is this if not an adventure?

                    ETHAN
This is not what I had in mind.

                    RICHARD (O.C.)
Just give me a few months, Ethan. A year at most.

                         ETHAN
              One year?

                         RICHARD (O.C.)
              Less. Give me a chance to
              avenge my death, to make
              those thugs pay. After that,
              I'm gone.

ETHAN again raises his leg to step off the bridge.

                         ETHAN
              I don't think so.

                         RICHARD (O.C.)
              WAIT! Wait. I promise --
              for once in your miserable
              life, you will actually *live*.
              (Beat). Light or life, Ethan,
              it's your choice. But
              remember, eternity will
              always be waiting for you.

INT. DR. TANNER'S OFFICE - NEXT DAY

ETHAN sits on Tanner's desk smoking and leafing
through a copy of *Journal of the American Medical
Association*.

The door opens. DRS. TANNER and YOUNG enter.
TANNER's chair is in the low position.

                         DR. TANNER
              Good morning, Ethan. I hope
              you slept well last night. We
              have a lot of work to . . .

DR. TANNER sees the cigarette.

                         DR. TANNER (CONT'D)
              What the hell are you doing
              smoking?

                         ETHAN
              (With Richard's personality)
              The heart wants what the
              heart wants, Doc.

                         DR. TANNER
              This is a smoke free campus
              for God's sake!

                           54

                    ETHAN
          Listen, Doc, if it were just
          me, I'd snuff it out in a
          minute. But it's Richard.
          He's been bitching for it all
          morning.

ETHAN tosses the *JAMA* onto the desk and stands up.

                    ETHAN (CONT'D)
          In light of my situation, I
          think you ought to quit
          reading this rag.

                    DR. TANNER
          Yes. Well, we'll have to see
          about that, won't we? (Beat)
          Anyway, we're here to talk
          about possibilities for
          Richard's eradication, not to
          watch you throw your life
          away.

ETHAN leans on DR. TANNER's wheelchair and looks down
on him.

                    ETHAN

          That's the key to life, isn't
          it? The never-ceasing fight
          for survival. But look more
          closely and you'll realize
          it's just a skeleton key
          you're clinging to.

                    DR. TANNER
          (Irritated) Do you want to
          hear our proposal or not?

                    ETHAN
          Not particularly. You see,
          I've already made my
          decision.

                    DR. TANNER
          And?

ETHAN blows smoke in DR. TANNER's face.

                    ETHAN
          I'm keeping him.

INT. BARN - DAY

                    RICHARD (O.C.)
          The first thing we need to do
          is get you into shape.

MONTAGE SEQUENCE set to "Jump" by Van Halen.

ETHAN lifts a barbell made of pipe and buckets; does
push-ups, chin-ups, crunches; climbs a ladder to the
hay loft.

SOPHIA [the horse] watches ETHAN work out. ETHAN
crosses off days on a calendar, measuring his biceps,
jogs on dirt roads.

ETHAN does one-handed push-ups, runs. Finally he does
target practice with an old and beautiful Smith &
Wesson .44 six-shooter.

MUSIC ENDS.

INT. DR. TANNER'S OFFICE - NIGHT

SISTER RITA is alone in the office, most of her face
hidden by the computer. She is gazing at the screen

ANGLE ON Ethan's file on the computer screen.

Suddenly RITA stops, looks upward, and crosses
herself.

EXT. PITTSBURGH AIRPORT - DAY

Shot of a plane landing.

TITLE CARD: PITTSBURGH INTERNATIONAL AIRPORT: MOON,
PA.

INT. PITTSBURGH AIRPORT GATE - DAY

Shot of SISTER RITA, in habit, coming out of the jet
way.

INT. FOOD COURT/PITTSBURGH AIRPORT - DAY

SISTER RITA is seated at a table, alone. She has coffee.

PROF. NORWICH approaches RITA.

> NORWICH
> Hello, Sister.

> SISTER RITA
> I'm glad you came, sister.

It becomes obvious they are identical twins.

NORWICH sits down.

> NORWICH
> I can never resist seeing
> myself without make-up and
> dressed in black.

RITA and NORWICH chuckle.

> NORWICH (CONT'D)
> I assume you had some news
> that couldn't wait for
> Thanksgiving Dinner.

> SISTER RITA
> Yes. (Beat). Remember that
> series of dreams we had when
> we were eleven, the ones we
> were sure were prophetic?

> NORWICH
> Of course. On the first night
> you dreamed of a Native
> American man with two hearts.

> SISTER RITA
> I have seen him.

> NORWICH
> (Un-phased). And?

> SISTER RITA
> He's a heart transplant
> patient at Saint Vincent's.
> He hears the donor's voice in
> his head.

                    NORWICH
          Ahh. That explains it.
          (BEAT). Well, I have news of
          my own. Remember *my* first
          dream in the series?

                    SISTER RITA
          You dreamed something, an
          object, struck the earth.
          That it was contact from
          another life form in the
          galaxy. You've been
          searching for it for years.

NORWICH smiles.

                    SISTER RITA (CONT'D)
          And you've found it?

                    NORWICH
          I'm not sure yet, but I think
          so. My tech and I will know
          within a week or two.

                    SISTER RITA
          Oh my. That means ...

                    NORWICH
          ... the other dreams we had
          ...

                    SISTER RITA
          ... that week are our future.

                    NORWICH
          Yes. Which means ...

                    SISTER RITA
          ... we have work to do.

INT. ETHAN'S BEDROOM - NIGHT

ETHAN and BEV are in bed in afterglow. She lays her
head and blond hair on his scarred chest. She pokes
his belly.

                    BEVERLY
          Your abs are really firm now.
          Those workouts are paying
          off.

                    ETHAN
          Thanks.

                    58

                    BEVERLY
You don't have a new
girlfriend do you? When a guy
starts working out ...

                    ETHAN
Nope. Just the same old
brunette.

                    BEVERLY
ETHAN!

                    ETHAN
Kidding! I just decided the
doctors were right about
taking better care of myself.
As you say: New Heart. New
Start.

                    BEVERLY
Good for you. And the
writing?

                    ETHAN
I'm writing some every day.

                    BEVERLY
When do I get to read it?

                    ETHAN
When the whole story is
written down. I'm driving up
to Columbus tomorrow for
research.

                    BEVERLY
Can you at least tell me what
you're writing?

                    ETHAN
A memoir. About life after a
heart transplant.

                    BEVERLY
Really? Is there much you
can say about that?

ETHAN gently cups one of Beverly's breasts.

                    ETHAN
More than you can imagine.

ETHAN and BEVERLY kiss and start making love.

EXT. COLUMBUS, OH - DAY

MUSIC for Columbus scenes: "Sorrow" by Pink Floyd.

ETHAN, in duster coat, walks through uptown Columbus.

> RICHARD (O.C.)
> Just before Ahab killed me, I
> discovered a weakness in his
> security: he's a creature of
> habit. One of his habits is
> coming to Columbus the first
> few days of each month to do
> business. He always stays at
> the same hotel and in the
> same suite.

ETHAN walks toward THE RENAISSANCE HOTEL

> RICHARD (O.C.)(CONT'D)
> Ahab is part of the Golden
> Crescent. His heroin supply
> comes from Afghanistan,
> crosses northern Iran - where
> he still has family - and
> into Turkey. From there it
> goes to Detroit then south to
> Columbus. Here he sells it to
> various dealers, and it
> supplies the entire
> Southeast.

ETHAN enters the Renaissance Hotel, sits in the lobby.

> ETHAN (V.O.)
>
> I thought all the heroin came
> from Mexico these days.

> RICHARD (O.C.)
> Ahab serves a wealthier
> cliental with much better
> product. The feds turn a
> blind eye because Ahab plans
> use the money to overthrow
> the Iranian government and
> make himself president. In
> exchange, he says he will
> turn the nuclear program over
> to the USA, though I can't
> imagine that really
> happening. It's all
> diplomatic poker.

60

DREADS and ALLYSON step off the elevator and walk past
ETHAN.

                    RICHARD (O.C.)(CONT'D)
               Ahab always travels with his
               girlfriend, Allyson.
               Everyday, she leaves the
               hotel at about 10 to go
               shopping, visit spas, and so
               on. A bodyguard always goes
               with her. That will leave
               Ahab and one other guard in
               the room.

ETHAN stands, walks to the elevator, then steps on.

INT. ELEVATOR CAR - DAY

MUSIC CONTINUES.

                    ETHAN (V.O.)
               I don't know if I can do
               this, Richard.

                    RICHARD (O.C.)
               Sure you can. Remember our
               agreement. And remember
               these are bad men. 1000s of
               people are dying from their
               drugs. For the so-called
               Greater Good.

Elevator bell DINGS.

INT. HOTEL HALLWAY/ROOM - DAY

MUSIC PAUSES.

ETHAN approaches the door to room 1102.

                    RICHARD (O.C.)
               Just like we rehearsed and do
               what I tell you. Knock.

ETHAN draws his gun from under his coat. He starts to
knock, stalls, takes a deep breath, and then finally
KNOCKS.

Long pause. The door opens to reveal AHAB in a white
bathrobe.

ETHAN rushes AHAB and pins him to a wall with his arm
at the throat. He then aims the gun at a THUG [a white
man] sitting by a window.

THUG tries to grab his own gun, but it's too late.

ETHAN shoots. THUG'S head is blown to bits. The window
shatters in a mix of blood and bits of skull and
brain.

[SCREENBOOK NOTE: This is the halfway point of the
film, and the only people to die, so far, have been
white. This an equal opportunity film.]

With his foot, ETHAN closes the door behind him and
puts the gun to AHAB'S head.

                    AHAB
               There's money on the desk.
               Take it all.

ETHAN in a voice that sounds a bit like RICHARD'S:

                    ETHAN
               Who ordered the hit on
               Richard Hamlin?

                    AHAB
               Who?

                    ETHAN
               The FBI agent you murdered in
               DC. Who set him up?

ETHAN cocks the gun.

                    AHAB
               It was his boss. William
               Spearing.

                    RICHARD (O.C.)
               That's all we need.

ETHAN moves the gun to aim it at AHAB'S heart.

                    AHAB
               Wait! Who sent you? We can
               deal.

                    ETHAN
               Richard sent me. No deals.

62

ETHAN fires twice. AHAB'S body slams into the wall.
Blood wells up through the white robe.

ETHAN rushes to the desk with stacks of money and
shovels the bills into his coat pockets.

ETHAN turns to leave, but hears the lock CLICK in the
door.

ETHAN ducks behind the door. DREADS enters.

> DREADS
> So guess what? Allyson forgot
> her purse ... (Sees Ahab's
> body) What the fuck?!

ALLYSON enters, rushes to AHAB'S body. She SCREAMS.

> ALLYSON
> OH GOD! NO!

DREADS rushes to the body of the THUG.

ETHAN slips from behind the door and rushes out, but
DREADS catches a glimpse of ETHAN and follows.

EXT/INT. <u>FOOT CHASE</u> - HOTEL/COLUMBUS - DAY

Pink Floyd's "Sorrow" begins PLAYING again.

ETHAN runs down the hallway to a fire escape. DREADS
follows and gains.

ETHAN runs through a conference room full of people.
ETHAN fires his third shot into the air. PEOPLE panic,
push, run, trample.

ETHAN rushes through the lobby and out into the
COLUMBUS streets. THUG #2 stands by a limo. ETHAN runs
down the street. DREADS rushes out, points to ETHAN.

> DREADS
> (To Thug #2). He killed Ahab!

ETHAN turns around, aims, fires shot 4. THUG #2 goes
down.

ETHAN runs again. Police SIRENS WAIL. DREADS chases
him until he reaches a fence and climbs over it into:

EXT. RAILYARDS - DAY

MUSIC CONT.

                    RICHARD (O.C.)
               Careful. This where they make
               up trains. These cars can
               move at anytime and on
               gravity. They don't make much
               noise.

A lethal game of hide-and-seek ensues between ETHAN
and DREADS among the various rolling stock. Shots
fired, both men out of bullets, DREADS pulls out his
razor.

They are about to fight on a set of tracks at the end
of a boxcar. ETHAN keeps backing up. A boxcar quietly
rolls up behind DREADS. Gravity brings them all
together.

The sound of SIRENS grows in volume and number.

ETHAN flings himself off the tracks just as a coupling
strikes DREADS in the back and shoves him forward and
downward so that his chest is crushed between the
couplings.

                    RICHARD (O.C.)
               Smashing.

MUSIC ENDS.

As ETHAN leaves the scene, KAREN, an ethnic woman with
black hair, peers, unseen, out of a boxcar.

                    KAREN
               (To herself). Shit! This was
               supposed to be my hit. I
               don't know who you are,
               asshole, but you're next.

INT. FARMHOUSE - NIGHT

BEVERLY is watching a news report about the shootings
in Columbus. Police have no leads.

ETHAN enters wearing his duster.

                         BEVERLY
              Oh, Ethan. I'm so glad
              you're home! Were you near
              the shootings?

                         ETHAN
              I heard the sirens, otherwise
              ...

ETHAN shrugs.

                         BEVERLY
              And you left your iPhone at
              home.

                         ETHAN
              Yeah. I didn't mean to. Just
              slipped my mind, you know.

ETHAN and BEVERLY kiss.

                         BEVERLY
              I was so worried. After all
              we've been through, I
              couldn't imagine losing you
              to such violence.

ETHAN and BEVERLY kiss again. It becomes frantic and
passionate. ETHAN sweeps BEVERLY off her feet.

                         BEVERLY
              ETHAN! You've never carried
              me to bed before.

                         ETHAN
              Then it's long overdue.

INT. ETHAN'S BEDROOM - NIGHT

MUSIC: "Fantasy" by Aldo Nova.

A SCENE OF SURREAL AND ANIMALISTIC SEX.

[Reader's choice: R or X rated]

Memories of the day and the images of night roil
together in ETHAN'S mind: BEVERLY'S body in the
shower, the bodies of AHAB's MEN, BEVERLY kissing
ETHAN'S body, blood on AHAB'S ROBE, nails digging into
a back, ALLYSON'S SCREAMS, blood flows from DREAD'S
mouth, BEVERLY MOANS, AHAB'S dead eyes, BEVERLY
SHRIEKS with pleasure, a bolt hitting his neck, the

headboard bangs the wall, and the car plunges off the
parking garage.

FADE TO BLACK

INT. BARN - DAY

ETHAN dumps Ahab's money into a box, pockets a few
bills, then places the box in a hole in the floor.
SOPHIA watches.

ETHAN covers the hole and pushes an old tractor over
the spot. He then sits down and lights a Camel
cigarette.

                    RICHARD (O.C.)
          You realize you are set for
          life now. That money is your
          bounty for killing my
          killers.

                    ETHAN
          Yes.

                    RICHARD (O.C.)
          You don't seem enthusiastic -
          - or thankful.

                    ETHAN
          No.

                    RICHARD (O.C.)
          Why?

                    ETHAN
          You already know.

                    RICHARD (O.C.)
          It helps when you articulate
          your thoughts.

                    ETHAN
          (Sighs). You are still
          spreading in my body. You
          feel everything I feel now.
          (Beat). There's no way I
          could have done all that in
          Columbus. You put me on some
          sort of auto-pilot to kill.

                    RICHARD (O.C.)
          Yes. I confess.

                    ETHAN
          You felt that boxcar moving
          on the tracks. That's what
          saved me.

                    RICHARD (O.C.)
          Yes.

                    ETHAN
          You feel the cool barn air
          now.

                    RICHARD (O.C.)
          Yes.

                    ETHAN
          And you felt my wife last
          night.

                    RICHARD (O.C.)
          No. Not that.

                    ETHAN
          Liar! I have never made love
          - had sex like that. Hell. I
          didn't feel it was me.

                    RICHARD (O.C.)
          No.

                    ETHAN
          You fucked my wife.

                    RICHARD (O.C.)
          No. I would never go that ...

                    ETHAN
          (Interrupting) Just shut.
          The. Fuck. Up.

                    RICHARD (O.C.)
          But ...

                    ETHAN
          (Interrupting) SILENCE!

EXT. DIRT ROAD - DAY

ETHAN rides SOPHIA through a wooded area.

They approach a little cottage. Chickens freely strut
around the yard.

EXT. COTTAGE - DAY

UNCLE JOHN, a Cherokee man, is chopping wood, sees
ETHAN and SOPHIA ride up. JOHN wears a T-shirt that
reads: FBI - Fry Bread Inspector.

                    JOHN
          Si-yo, nephew.

                    ETHAN
          O-si-yo, John.

JOHN hugs and steadies SOPHIA as ETHAN climbs down.

                    JOHN
          Si-yo, Sophia-Carrot-Thief.

                    ETHAN
          You taught her.

JOHN and ETHAN hug.

                    JOHN
          Did they give you a pair of
          new legs with that heart?

                    ETHAN
          No. Why?

                    JOHN
          'Cause you're taller, enit.

                    ETHAN
          Nah. You're just trying to
          make up a new story.

                    JOHN
          (Laughing). Nah, man you're a
          foot taller - or maybe an
          inch. I ain't decided yet.
          (Beat) Come on in. Granny'll
          be glad to see you.

INT. COTTAGE LIVING/DINING/KITCHEN AREA - DAY

The front room is lined with shelves full of native
and non-native curiosities.

A round table fills the central space. A basket full
of eggs rests at the center of the table.

GRANNY is sitting at the table. She is an old
Cherokee woman and full of life, an elder familiar
with the world.

                    GRANNY
          Is that Ethan come to see his
          Granny?

                    JOHN
          Sure is, mama.

                    ETHAN
          Si-yo, Granny.

                    GRANNY
          Ethan! Come and sit with me a
          spell.

ETHAN sits next to GRANNY. She is grinding up some
herbs.

                    GRANNY (CONT'D)
          Say. Did you hear about them
          bad men who got killed up in
          Columbus yesterday?

                    ETHAN
          Um. Yeah. Yeah I did. Why?

                    GRANNY
          It's an awful thing, ya know.

                    ETHAN
          Yes. It is.

                    GRANNY
          And do you know when Columbus
          was incorporated as a city?

                    ETHAN
          No idea, Granny.

                    GRANNY
          1492.

ETHAN and JOHN laugh.

                    JOHN
          You been waiting' all day to
          tell that joke, enit mama?

                    GRANNY
          Yes I have. (Beat). Let me
          fix you boys some dinner. Or

                    69

lunch. Or whatever it is they
call it now-a-days.

INT. LIVING/DINING/KITCHEN AREA - DAY

GRANNY, ETHAN, and JOHN all dig in to their lunch:
Fried chicken, green beans, cornbread, and milk.

>   GRANNY
> So Ethan, how you gettin' on
> with that heart they gave ya?

>   ETHAN
> Healthiest I've been since I
> was about 20.

>   GRANNY
> Well, you sure look better
> than when I seen you in that
> hospital.

>   ETHAN
> I'm sure I do.

>   JOHN
> He's taller, too. A good two
> inches.

>   GRANNY
> I seen that. Part of it is on
> account he's standing
> straighter, but he's growed a
> bit, too. I reckon that's to
> be expected. A change of
> heart should bring on a few
> other changes, enit.

>   ETHAN
> I don't know about my height,
> but yeah, it's changed me.

>   GRANNY
> (In Cherokee). All that lives
> must change to survive.

>   ETHAN
> Sorry. All I caught was
> "lives" and "survive."

>   GRANNY
> To survive you gotta change.
> (Beat) White people look at
> a rock on the ground and call

70

it dead. But it lives, it
lives forever. It changes
though, what with the
weather. Water wears it down,
smooths it up. That rock
teaches us things like
patience for great change --
or disaster, like when
lightening hits it. But even
then it becomes many
beautiful rocks.

> ETHAN
> I guess you're right.

> GRANNY
> The *Tsalagi* were once a great
> rock. Now we're many smaller
> stones scattered across the
> land. But you know what?
> *Unelanvhi*, God, is in every
> rock, and so he is inside
> every one of us.

> ETHAN
> That's a lot to take in.

> GRANNY
> I can see that a great change
> has come over you, Ethan.
> You're not sure about the
> future. Just remember this.
> Follow God's path even though
> you don't know where it
> leads, because in the end, it
> always leads you to the heart
> of the universe.

EXT. DIRT ROAD - DAY

ETHAN rides SOPHIA back home.

> ETHAN
> Old Granny was right, Sophia.
> (Beat). Richard is going to
> start hounding me about
> killing his boss for him, and
> I have got to say no. It
> isn't right, such a thing.
> Not at all. And if you heard
> that, Richard, I mean it.
> This is the end.

INT. FARMHOUSE ENTRYWAY - DAY

ETHAN casually walks in his front door only to find a
gun aimed at his forehead.

ETHAN freezes.

                    RICHARD(O.C.)
          Ethan, meet Karen.

KAREN holds the gun steady. She studies Ethan's face a
moment.

                    KAREN
          Why did you kill Ahab and his
          men? Tell me!

ETHAN's voice sounds more like RICHARD's:

                    ETHAN
          I was greatly afflicted: I
          said in my haste: All men are
          liars. (Beat). Psalm 116

KAREN lowers her gun slightly.

                    KAREN
          You knew Richard?

                    ETHAN
          Yeah.

                    KAREN
          He used to say that whenever
          things got screwy.

                    ETHAN
          Yes. He does. Did.

                    KAREN
          You were avenging his death?

                    ETHAN
          Yes.

                    KAREN
          That was my job. Richard and
          I were a thing, a couple. I
          would have died for him.
          Then, the way he was
          butchered ...

                    ETHAN
          Ahab told me who set him up.

72

                    KAREN
          Spearing?

                    ETHAN
          Spearing.

                    KAREN
          I'm not surprised. Spearing
          is part of some top-secret
          thing the FBI has with NASA.
          He was also jealous of us.

                    ETHAN
          So it's not over yet?

                    KAREN
          No. Not even.

                    ETHAN
          Then we have work to do.

INT. PROF. NORWICH'S OFFICE - DAY

NORWICH works at her desk. The desk is covered with
papers, and resting on top of those are five blue
robotic butterflies in various stages of disrepair.

NORWICH is "dissecting" one.

NASIM walks into the office carrying an iPad.

                    NASIM
          Prof. Norwich, here's the
          latest. I thought you'd want
          to ...

NASIM stops to stare at the butterflies.

                    NASIM (CONT.)
          Those are Blue Morpho
          butterflies! They are only
          found in South and Central
          America. Are you a collector?

                    NORWICH
          Look closer.

NASIM steps closer and bends over to study them.

                    NASIM
          AH! They're not real?

                    73

                    NORWICH
          Oh, they're real all right.
          But they're not natural.
          They're some sort of bio-
          robotic hybrid.

                    NASIM
          But who? What?

                    NORWICH
          Exactly, Nasim. We know
          nothing about them, but at
          least a few dozen have been
          found around the world. China
          claims Russia is using them
          to spy with. Russia says
          we're making them. We
          aren't. None of us have this
          technology. And finally,
          we're not even sure what they
          are supposed to do. There's
          no camera and no transmitter
          that we can find.

                    NASIM
          So, why are you studying
          them? Isn't this more like
          FBI or CIA stuff?

                    NORWICH
          Because we think they may
          come from somewhere other
          than Earth. (Beat) They may
          be coming in these things we
          often find near the robots.

NORWICH reaches into a FEDEX box by her chair. She
pulls out a metal cylinder about 8 inches long and an
1½" in diameter. It has a glass lens on one end along
with wires and gadgets. It looks like the lovechild of
a spaceship and a flashlight.

NASIM stares in wonder, as NORWICH sets it in the
middle of the desk.

                    NASIM
          It's like some sort of bio-
          mechanical cocoon.

                    NORWICH
          Might need to add "extra-
          terrestrial" to that list.

                    NASIM
          Oh My God. I was just coming
          to show you this.

NASIM scrolls and swipes through her iPad a moment
then hands it to NORWHICH.

NORWICH studies it a moment.

ANGLE ON: iPad screen, a drawing of a "cocoon" very
similar to the one on Norwich's desk.

                    NORWICH
          Are you certain?

                    NASIM
          99 percent.

                    NORWICH
          If you'll excuse me, I need
          to make a few calls now.

                    NASIM
          Yes. I'll see what more I can
          find out there.

                    NORWICH
          Thank you, Nasim. And as
          before, this is classified
          information.

                    NASIM
          Yes, Dr. Norwich. Of course.

NASIM leaves. NORWICH dials a landline phone.

                    SPEARING (O.S.)
          You're using the wrong line.

                    NORWICH
          No I'm not.

                    SPEARING (O.S.)
          You have something.

                    NORWICH
          It is an object moving at a
          very high speed. It appears
          to be manufactured.

                    SPEARING (O.S.)
          Really? Where is it?

                          75

                    NORWICH
          Between Mars and earth.

                    SPEARING (O.S.)
          And you're sure it's not an
          asteroid or something -
          normal?

                    NORWICH
          Positive. It is symmetrical,
          and, as of this morning it
          appears to have charted a new
          course. (BEAT) It looks like
          one of those cocoons we've
          been finding, but it's damn
          near the size of a bus.

                    SPEARING (O.S.)
          (Pause) And?

                    NORWICH
          If it follows its current
          trajectory and speed, it will
          probably strike somewhere in
          North America. My tech will
          pinpoint the site as it
          approaches.

                    SPEARING (O.S.)
          The second one for North
          America. Our first real
          chance to study one. ETA?

                    NORWICH
          Ten days.

                    SPEARING (O.S.)
          Name?

NORWICH does a quick search on one of her computers.

                    NORWICH
          I'm going with an Intelligent
          Life Contact Designation, so
          it will be code named
          Heartbeat ... um,   seven.
          Heartbeat Seven.

                    SPEARING (O.S.)
          Good. I'll have the
          facilities prepped and proper
          clearances granted.

                        NORWICH
            I'll set up ETIC protocol and
            alert personnel as needed.

                        SPEARING (O.S.)
            Of course.

                        NORWICH
            And Spearing?

                        SPEARING (O.S.)
            What?

                        NORWICH
            Don't fuck this one up.

NORWICH hangs up.

INT. SPEARING'S STUDY - DAY

SPEARING shoots up heroin.

                        SPEARING
            (To himself) Woman's gotta be
            a damned witch the way she
            keeps finding these things.

SHOT of SPEARING'S face for the first time. He is
polished and handsome.

SPEARING closes his eyes, and his face changes to a
state of bliss as the heroin kicks in.

INT. FARMHOUSE KITCHEN - DAY

ETHAN and KAREN are seated at the table, drinking
coffee.

                        KAREN
            So in seven days you'll fly
            to DC.

                        ETHAN
            Right. And you're willing to
            be the bait?

                        KAREN
            Spearing trusts me. Hell, he

thinks he's in love with me.
I'm the best bet for luring
him out of his lair.

                    ETHAN
          So we have a plan.

                    KAREN
          A good plan.

                    ETHAN
          Okay. I hate to be rude, but
          my wife, she's a science
          teacher at the middle school
          just down the road, and
          she'll be coming home soon.

                    KAREN
          Oh. Of course, I better get
          scarce.

ETHAN and KAREN stand up. Suddenly she hugs him.

                    KAREN (O.S.)
          Thank you for doing this.

                    ETHAN
          Well, let's just say
          Richard's gotten under my
          skin.

EXT. LONG DRIVEWAY - DAY

KAREN's car makes its way down the gravel driveway and
out onto the highway.

KAREN pulls onto the highway just in time for BEVERLY,
in her own car, to see KAREN.

BEVERLY is suspicious.

EXT. OUTER SPACE

SHOT of HEARTBEAT-SEVEN, the
flashlight/cocoon/spaceship, hurtling through space
and toward earth.

EXT. FARM YARD - DAY

ETHAN brushes SOPHIA - and smokes a Camel.

                    ETHAN
          I'm not really sure I can go
          through with this plan to
          kill your boss, Richard. This
          isn't who I am.

                    RICHARD (O.C.)
          Then think of it as being a
          Warrior. A Cherokee warrior.
          Like your ancestors.

                    ETHAN
          Really? You're argument is to
          pull some racist stereotype
          out for me to bow down to?
          I'm not a warrior. And while
          we're at it, buddy. Don't
          think I haven't noticed the
          fact that my skin, eyes, and
          hair are getting lighter.

                    RICHARD (O.C.)
          What are you saying?

                    ETHAN
          I'm saying that you are
          colonizing my body. You are
          invading every part of me. I
          even had feelings for your
          girlfriend yesterday. That's
          why I agreed to kill
          Spearing. Now I'm saying no.

                    RICHARD (O.C.)
          Well, it's not like you have
          that many years left anyway.

                    ETHAN
          What do you mean?

                    RICHARD (O.C.)
          I mean most heart transplant
          patients only live about 5 or
          10 years anyway.

                    ETHAN
          You're lying.

                    RICHARD (O.C.)
The doctors lied. Medicine
and mendacity walk hand-in-
hand. You only have about a
50 percent chance of making
it 10 years. Living to a
ripe old age isn't in your
cards, buddy. And now that
you're smoking whenever you
can ...

                    ETHAN
Go away. I want to be alone.

                    RICHARD (O.C.)
And you can be sure Bev is
making plans for post-Ethan
life.

                    ETHAN
Just go away.

A car rolls up the drive. DR. YOUNG is driving.

DR. YOUNG parks and gets out.

                    ETHAN
(To himself). Shit. What now?

                    DR. YOUNG
Hey, Ethan. This is a nice
place you have here.

                    ETHAN
You making house calls these
days, Doc?

                    DR. YOUNG
Not often, no. But you're a
special case.

                    ETHAN
Am I?

                    DR. YOUNG
Yes. And you haven't come to
see me in a while. I thought
I better check on you.

                    ETHAN
Well - I was about to walk
Sophia here a bit. You can
walk along if you want.

                        80

                    DR. YOUNG
          Sure.

ETHAN slips a rope lead on the horse, and they walk
out a path through a wooded area.

                    ETHAN
          So what did you want to know?

                    DR. YOUNG
          Let's start with Richard. You
          continue to look different.
          I assume he's still
          spreading?

                    ETHAN
          Yes.

                    DR. YOUNG
          We really should be
          documenting these changes.

                    ETHAN
          Why?

                    DR. YOUNG
          For future reference,
          research.

                    ETHAN
          I suppose, but nah. It'd just
          be more and more questions.
          It'd never end. I just want
          to be left alone, remember?

                    DR. YOUNG
          I remember. (Beat) I have
          done more research on your
          anomaly. A lot more.
          There's a woman in Germany
          with multiple personalities.
          One of her personalities is
          allergic to bread. She
          breaks out in hives, but the
          hives disappear as she
          changes to another
          personality. Curious, isn't
          it?

                    ETHAN
          What are you trying to tell
          me?

                    DR. YOUNG
          The mind is exceedingly
          powerful. It creates your
          reality. We just need to
          learn how to control it.

PAUSE in talking. An EAGLE SCREECHES. ETHAN and DR.
YOUNG search the sky. ETHAN points out the soaring
bird.

                    ETHAN
          I don't know who I am any
          more, Doc. *What* I am. I'm not
          sure where Richard begins and
          where I end.

                    DR. YOUNG
          I can only try to imagine.
          (Beat). I've also found two
          cases similar to yours. One
          in South Africa. The other in
          Argentina.

                    ETHAN
          What happened to them?

                    DR. YOUNG
          They each committed suicide
          within two years of their
          transplant.

                    ETHAN
          (Chuckling). Richard talked
          me out of it. Now he
          controls so much of my body,
          I'm not sure I could pull it
          off.

                    DR. YOUNG
          I see. (Beat). Have you ever
          told Beverly?

                    ETHAN
          No.

                    DR. YOUNG
          Why not?

                    ETHAN
          She'd treat me like a science
          experiment, probably push for
          a mechanical heart. Make me
          the world's first Indian
          Cyborg.

                        82

DR. YOUNG smiles.

                    DR. YOUNG
          Still, wouldn't it be nice to
          have someone to confide in,
          so you won't feel alone.

                    ETHAN
          That's the problem, Dr.
          Young. I'm never alone.

ETHAN, DR. YOUNG, and SOPHIA return to the barn area
just as BEVERLY pulls up in her own car.

BEV steps out and runs her fingers through her hair.

                    BEVERLY
          Hello, Dr. Young. What brings
          you out this way?

                    DR. YOUNG
          Just a little house call -
          and exercise with a horse.
          Always wanted one. And a
          farm like this. It's nice
          here. Peaceful.

ETHAN sees a spark between BEVERLY and DR. YOUNG.

                    BEVERLY
          It's one of the reasons I
          hooked up with this *old* guy
          in the first place.

                    ETHAN
          All we need now is a new dog.

Nervous LAUGHTER all around.

Dr. YOUNG moves toward his car.

                    DR. YOUNG
          Well, I guess I'll be shoving
          off.

                    BEVERLY
          What? Wouldn't you like to
          stay for supper?

                    DR. YOUNG
          No, thank you. Maybe some
          other time, but I'm needed
          back at the hospital. Rounds
          to make.

                    ETHAN
          Thanks for the check-up.

                    DR. YOUNG
          No problem, Ethan. Just
          consider some of what I told
          you and let me know what I
          can do for you.

DR. YOUNG starts his car and pulls away.

                    DR. YOUNG
          Bye.

                    ETHAN
          Good-bye.

                    BEVERLY
          Be careful driving back.

ETHAN and BEVERLY are left alone.

                    BEVERLY (CONT'D)
          So what did he really want?

                    ETHAN
          Um, he wants me to join him
          at a conference or seminar
          thing next week in DC.
          Something about depression
          and recovery in transplant
          cases.

                    BEVERLY
          Are you going?

                    ETHAN
          Yes. I am.

ETHAN turns away to lead SOPHIA back to the barn.

ETHAN glances back to see BEVERLY longingly follow Dr.
Young's car with her eyes.

FADE TO BLACK

INT. NORWICH'S OFFICE - DAY

NASIM and PROF. NORWICH peer at a computer screen full
of numbers.

NASIM

... and here is where it
seemed to adjust its course
again. It appears to be
targeting earth. It has to be
an Extra Terrestrial ship or
probe.

NORWICH

Where's the projected strike
zone at this time?

NASIM

The Maine and Canadian
border, but this is no
asteroid. It could still make
adjustments. If it slows
down, that zone would be
farther west and, possibly,
south.

NORWICH

Yes. I know.

NASIM

I only hope it hits some
remote place. That thing
could kill a lot of people.

NORWICH

OK, NASIM. Here's what I want
you to do. Go home. Get some
rest. Pack your things for an
extended trip. At 0800, you
and I will meet up here and
leave for ETIC to prepare for
HEARTBEAT-SEVEN to land in
our backyard.

NASIM

Professor Norwich? Forgive
me if I'm being dense, but
what is ETIC?

NORWICH

The Extra Terrestrial
Investigation Center.
Congratulations, Nasim. I
just gave you Top Secret
Clearance. After this is all
over, you can go to AREA 52.

INT. FARMHOUSE KITCHEN - NIGHT

ETHAN and BEVERLY eat dinner in silence until BEVERLY
YAWNS.

                    BEVERLY
          Geez. I don't know why I'm
          so tired tonight.

                    ETHAN
          You do deal with pubescent
          children all day. That'd
          wear me out.

                    BEVERLY
          True. But you seem to have
          more energy lately.

                    ETHAN
          New Heart. New Start - as you
          say.

                    BEVERLY
          Have you thought about
          looking for a new job? I
          mean, I know you're writing
          and keeping house and all,
          but maybe it's time to think
          about more income.

                    ETHAN
          I guess I should. I will when
          I get back from DC.

Pause.

                    BEVERLY
          Where are you really going?

                    ETHAN
          I told you. Washington. The
          conference for Dr. Young.

                    BEVERLY
          You're lying. I can tell.

                    ETHAN
          Say what?

                    BEVERLY
          You're lying. You'll be
          screwing your new, raven-
          headed girlfriend somewhere.

                    ETHAN
          You've got to be kidding!

                    BEVERLY
          Working out. Lightening your
          hair. Better posture. More
          energy. I've watched my
          students enough to know when
          they're turned on by someone
          new.

                    ETHAN
          Like the way you acted around
          Dr. Young today? You might
          as well have been full-on
          flirting. "Wouldn't you like
          to stay for supper, kind
          Doctor Young, so very young
          man?"

                    BEVERLY
          I was being hospitable, you
          dolt.

                    ETHAN
          New Life. New Wife.

          BEVERLY slaps ETHAN.

                    BEVERLY
          That woman I saw leaving the
          house the other day, she
          going to be your new wife?

                    ETHAN
          What?

                    BEVERLY
          That's right. I saw her.

                    ETHAN
          That was some college kid
          selling magazine
          subscriptions.

                    BEVERLY
          She hardly looked the part.
          She looked like a cheap
          whore.

                    ETHAN
          (In RICHARD'S voice). Don't
          you ever call her that.

PAUSE.

                    BEVERLY
          That's what I thought.

BEVERLY is pale and hunches over.

BEVERLY rushes to the kitchen sink and throws up her
dinner, and lunch.

ETHAN rushes to her side, pulls back her hair.

                    BEVERLY (CONT'D)
          Don't. You. Touch. Me.

ETHAN leaves the kitchen as the PUKING continues.

INT. FARMHOUSE - NIGHT

ETHAN tries to get comfortable to sleep on the couch.

                    ETHAN (V.O.)
          Thanks a lot, Richard.

                    RICHARD (O.C.)
          When you seek adventure, you
          find yourself sleeping on a
          lot of different couches.
          Just saying.

EXT. OUTER SPACE

SHOT of HEARTBEAT-SEVEN. Small rockets on its sides
move. Brief bursts of flames leap out of the rockets
in silence.

HEARTBEAT-SEVEN re-adjusts its course toward earth.

INT./EXT. DC DULLES AIRPORT - NIGHT

MUSIC: "The Groove is in the Heart" by Dee Lite.

Surrounded by throngs of people, ETHAN exits a gate
area and walks though the airport.

ETHAN looks even more like RICHARD.

ETHAN has new, stylish clothes, and there is a
confident swagger to his walk.

ETHAN walks, with a carry-on bag, through the terminal
and out the door.

ETHAN jumps into a cab.

EXT. WASHINGTON, DC - NIGHT

MUSIC CONT.

SHOTS of ETHAN'S cab passing familiar landmarks. Cab
pulls up in front of the luxurious Sofitel Hotel.

INT./EXT. SOFITEL HOTEL - NIGHT

MUSIC CONT.

SHOTS of ETHAN checking in.

ETHAN flirts at a bar, floats in a roof-top pool.

INT. HOTEL HALLWAY - MORNING

MUSIC CONT.

KAREN walks down the hallway. KNOCKS on a room door.

MUSIC STOPS.

ETHAN opens the door, wearing nothing but a towel
around his waist. ETHAN now looks and SOUNDS a lot
like RICHARD.

                    ETHAN
          Good morning, Karen. Come in.

KAREN, a bit transfixed, enters.

INT. POSH HOTEL ROOM - MORNING

                    KAREN
          I thought you were going to
          stay at the Holiday Inn?

                    ETHAN
          This was more to my liking.

                    KAREN
          You sound like Richard.

                    ETHAN
          We shared many things.

                    KAREN
          I see. Well.

KAREN looks at the messy bed.

                    KAREN (CONT'D)
          Sleep well?

                    ETHAN
          Like the dead.

KAREN pulls a RUGER 9mm gun from her purse.

                    KAREN
          Here's the gun. I think
          it'll be better than that
          canon you blasted Columbus
          with.

ETHAN takes the gun.

                    ETHAN
          Thank you.

KAREN pulls out a piece of paper.

                    KAREN
          And here's the address. It's
          a used bookstore with a café
          in the back. We're supposed
          to meet at 2, so walk in
          about 2:10. Then. You know
          what to do. I'll have a gun
          in case things go south.

                    ETHAN
          We'll try to avoid that.

                    KAREN
          And then, I suppose, we go
          opposite directions. I'll
          call you in a day or two to
          check on you. Got it?

                    ETHAN
          Yes.

                    KAREN
          Okay. Then I'll see you
          there.

                    ETHAN
          Maybe you'd like to stay here
          a while. Order room service.

Pause.

                    KAREN
          That sounds wonderful, but...

                    ETHAN
          But?

                    KAREN
          I need to take care of a few
          things. I plan to disappear
          for a few months after this.

KAREN steps closer.

                    ETHAN
          Not from me I hope.

                    KAREN
          It's so strange. I feel like
          I'm with Richard when I see
          you. You even smell like
          him.

                    ETHAN
          Maybe you'll disappear in my
          direction.

                    KAREN
          Do you mean that?

                    ETHAN
          I do.

                    KAREN
          What about your wife?

                    ETHAN
          We've … separated.

KAREN and ETHAN kiss. Karen backs away, to the door,
unsure what's going on.

                    KAREN
          I'll see you at the store.

INT. USED BOOK STORE - DAY

SPEARING and KAREN sit at a cafe table. SPEARING has
an early copy of *Dune* at hand.

                    KAREN
          Still spending the family
          fortune on old books, I see.

                    SPEARING
          Yes.

                    KAREN
          With all that money, why work
          for the FBI?

                    SPEARING
          Life is a game. You must
          play at something. (Beat)
          It's a good thing you came
          today. I'm about to leave
          town for quite some time.

                    KAREN
          Business?

                    SPEARING
          Yes. An investment is about
          to pay off.

A bell on the front door RINGS. ETHAN/RICHARD enters.

                    SPEARING (CONT'D)
          I wish you would come with
          me. It's an exciting
          development, a game changer.

                    KAREN
          Is that a good thing?

                    SPEARING
          We'll soon see. But if you
          stay with me, I can assure
          your safety.

                      92

ETHAN'S shadow falls on SPEARING. SPEARING looks up.

                    SPEARING (CONT'D)
          RICHARD? It can't be.

KAREN stands and backs away from the table.

                    KAREN
          You can't even save yourself.

SPEARING stands.

ETHAN draws his gun, aims at SPEARING's head.

                    ETHAN
          Vengeance is mine, thus saith
          the Lord.

ETHAN lowers the gun to aim at SPEARING'S heart and
fires twice. SPEARING's body flings back into a pastry
case. CRASH!

ETHAN and KAREN quickly turn and head for the door.

Halfway through the store a bullet whizzes by ETHAN's
head.

ETHAN and KAREN look back to see SPEARING crawling out
of the debris, his gun drawn.

                    KAREN
          The son-of-a-bitch is wearing
          his ballistic vest.

A firefight erupts. Patrons seek cover. Books blast
off the shelves like dying pigeons.

Behind a counter, the SHOPKEEPER pulls out a shotgun,
but he's not sure whom to shoot. He blasts a shot
into the air.

From opposite ends, KAREN and SPEARING both shoot THE
SHOPKEEPER.

ETHAN shoots SPEARING in the arm. SPEARING rushes into
the back of the store. SIRENS begin to wail.

ETHAN starts after SPEARING. KAREN stops him.

                    KAREN
          There's no time. We have to
          leave.

                    ETHAN
          But.

                    KAREN
          He'll trap you in the alley.

                    ETHAN
          It doesn't matter.

                    KAREN
          Whoever you are, I can't lose
          you a second time.

Hesitantly ETHAN and KAREN retreat out the front door
and head in opposite directions.

EXT. DC STREETS - DAY

ETHAN drops the gun in a storm sewer, finds a cab, and
gets in.

INT. CAB - MOVING - DAY

                    ETHAN
              (To Cabbie) Dulles Airport

PAUSE

                    ETHAN (CONT'D)(V.O.)
          I'm sorry, Richard. Richard?

INT. ETIC WAREHOUSE - DAY

Large black trucks and RV's are warming up to pullout.

NORWICH walks along an RV. NASIM sticks her head out a
window.

                    NASIM
          It's headed for south-east
          Tennessee. It's changing
          course like it's looking for
          a specific place.

                    NORWICH
          Maybe it is. ETA?

                       94

                         NASIM
          2100.

                         NORWICH
          Let's roll.

NORWICH boards the RV as the trucks begin moving and a
large garage door opens.

INT. FARMHOUSE - EVENING

ETHAN enters his house weary and anxious.

                         ETHAN
               Bev? Bev? You home?

ETHAN finds a note on the table.

ANGLE ON Note: It reads: Ethan. I've gone to a
friend's house for a few days to sort my mind. - Bev.

                         ETHAN
               (Frustrated) Great.

ETHAN grabs a bottle of bourbon from a cabinet.
Drinks from the bottle, lights a cigarette.

ETHAN/RICHARD have a psychotic conversation. ETHAN's
lips move but the voices come from between ETHAN and
RICHARD.

                         ETHAN/RICHARD
               You realize Beverly is done
               with you. Yes I am. The FBI
               will find that gun and your
               hotel room. They will find
               you. Us. They will find us.
               Yes. Us. Spearing will hide
               in his little book room,
               shoot up heroin from
               Afghanistan, and we will rot
               in prison. That seems fair.

Pause. Then, in two distinct voices, ETHAN and RICHARD
SCREAM. ETHAN heaves the bottle across the room.
CRASH.

                            95

                    ETHAN/RICHARD (CONT'D)
          We are now outlaws. We have
          to leave. Get the hell outta
          Dodge. Yes. Yes. But first -
          we gotta leave the journal.
          First you need to finish it.
          Yes. Yes.

ETHAN sits at the computer and begins typing
furiously.

INT. FARMHOUSE - NIGHT

ETHAN is harried but still typing. A second bottle of
booze stands by the computer, empty.

ANGLE ON the computer screen: "Then after leaving a
print copy of this journal for you, Bev, I left for
regions unknown. The End."

                        ETHAN
          Best thing I've ever written.
          (BEAT) It's all over,
          Richard. All but the part
          about running for the rest of
          our lives. Richard? Richard?
          I see. Now *you* bail on me.
          Internal asshole.

ETHAN clicks "Print."

As the printer does its job, ETHAN stands, walks to
the couch, and falls onto it, asleep.

FADE TO BLACK

INT. FARMHOUSE - MORNING

ETHAN wakes up, hung over, slowly gets his bearings.

ETHAN collects his journal from the printer, tidies
the stack of paper, and sets it on the table, by Bev's
note.

ETHAN returns to the living room, picks up the remote,
and turns on the TV.

                          96

There's breaking news. The screen is filled with
images of a huge fire at a shopping mall.

At the bottom of the screen are the words: Hamilton
Mall: Chattanooga, TN.

> FEMALE REPORTER (V.O.)
> These are shots we took last
> night at about 10pm, just
> before the Air Force cleared
> the air space for ten miles
> around. As you can see, the
> fire was intense.

ETHAN is unimpressed, stretches, scratches his belly.

> REPORTER (V.O.) (CONT'D)
> Rumors about the cause are
> rampant. Was it terrorism?
> Was it an Air Force jet? At
> least one person who
> witnessed the impact thinks
> it was a UFO, if you can
> imagine. Here is footage from
> a dash cam.

TV shows a glowing streak across a night sky, then
BOOM!

> REPORTER (V.O.) (CONT'D)
> Most experts who have seen
> this video, suggest that it
> was a meteorite.

The TV image changes to a live feed of the reporter
standing at the police tape, smoke rises over her
shoulder.

> REPORTER (CONT'D)
> Witnesses say the object hit
> near the food court area,
> where, apparently, a Boy
> Scout troop was enjoying ice
> cream after seeing a movie.

> ETHAN
> (To himself) Rough night in
> old Chattanooga, too, I
> guess.

TV camera swings to a different angle. ETHAN squints
at the screen.

ANGLE ON shot of a black RV and black trucks. SPEARING
steps out of the RV.

> ETHAN (CONT'D)
> Spearing?

> RICHARD (O.C.)
> Spearing. He's left his lice
> den. This is big. And he'll
> be out in the open with a
> target on his butt.

ETHAN's phone BUZZES with a text.

KAREN: Are you watching the news?

ETHAN: Yes. And S is there.

KAREN: I'm already on the way. Meet you there?

ETHAN: Yes.

EXT. HAMILTON MALL - EVENING

TITLE CARD: CHATTANOOGA, TN

The mall ruins are ringed with TV trucks, reporters,
emergency vehicles, family members of missing loved
ones, the curious, police, and National Guard troops.

ETHAN and KAREN wind their way through the crowd and
slip under the yellow tape.

ETHAN and KAREN pick their way among the ETIC trucks
to get closer to the impact site.

Large lights illuminate the scene.

Smoke still rises from a large crater. Large cranes
approach.

WORKERS wear biohazard suits.

> ETHAN
> This is unreal.

> KAREN
> With ETIC here, it must be
> something from outer space,
> but they wouldn't take these
> precautions for a meteor.

                    ETHAN
          And this equipment, drug
          money paid for all this?

                    KAREN
          Yes, and I can think of at
          least one private investor.

                    ETHAN
          Spearing?

                    KAREN
          He's loaded and looking for
          more.

ETHAN and KAREN inch just close enough to see the top
of the object in the crater.

Then GUARD #1 appears behind them with a rifle.

                    GUARD #1
          Don't move. Slowly raise
          your hands.

GUARD #2 appears, pats ETHAN and KAREN down, takes
their guns.

                    GUARD #2
          Follow me.

The GUARDS escort ETHAN and KAREN to the ETIC RV.
GUARD #2 opens the door and steps in. The others
follow.

INT. ETIC RV - NIGHT

The RV is a command post full of hi-tech equipment.

NASIM and NORWICH are seated and studying screens with
images of the impact zone. As ETHAN and the camera
move, we see that the object in the crater does,
indeed, look like the "Cocoons," only huge.

SPEARING stands with his back turned, talking on his
phone.

                    SPEARING
          I expect us to roll with the
          cargo at 0700.

SPEARING clicks off the call and turns around.

                    SPEARING (CONT'D)
          (To Karen and Ethan) You two.
          I've been watching you for
          half an hour.

SPEARING points to TV screens showing various shots of
the crash site.

NORWICH stands and steps closer to hear.

                    SPEARING (CONT'D)
          What gives, Karen? You spying
          for the Chinese these days?
          That'll keep you in prison
          for life, you little
          turncoat.

                    KAREN
          You had Richard killed. What
          do you expect from me you
          miserable piece of shit? But
          it's just a game, right?

                    SPEARING
          Hmmm. (To Ethan). And you Hot
          Shot. Just who the hell are
          you?

                    ETHAN
          Richard Hamlin sent me.

                    SPEARING
          You look so much like him, I
          even double checked the
          records last night to make
          sure Richard didn't have a
          twin brother. (Beat) I'm
          curious; you had a bead on my
          head. Why did you shoot at
          my heart instead?

                    ETHAN
          I'm something of an authority
          on hearts.

                    SPEARING
          Oh gawd. He's a poet, just
          like Richard. (To Guard #2)
          Take him out, beat the shit
          out of him, and when he's
          dead dump his body in the
          rubble and set fire to it.
          Hot Shot just became a
          casualty of the "accident."

                         100

                    GUARD #2
          Sir?!

                    ETHAN
          Richard Hamlin is alive.
          I got his heart through a
          transplant. He lives in me. I
          hear his voice. Follow his
          lead.

KAREN GASPS. NORWICH steps closer.

                    NORWICH
          You were at Saint Vincent's,
          weren't you?

ETHAN studies NORWICH's face.

                    ETHAN
          Sister Rita?

NORWICH smiles.

                    NORWICH
          No. But you get the cigar
          anyway. Rita is my twin.

NORWICH backs away, smiling intently.

                    ETHAN
          What's going on here?

Ignoring ETHAN, NORWICH whispers into SPEARING'S ear.

                    SPEARING
          (More to himself than to
          Norwich). Oh Gawd. Alright.
          (To all present). I don't
          have time for this bullshit
          right now. (To Ethan and
          Karen) Apparently we're
          gonna have to use some
          enhanced interrogation
          techniques on the two of you.
          (To guards). Lock them both
          in the back of Truck Five,
          then keep two guards on that
          truck at all times.

                    GUARDS #1 & 2
          Yes, sir.

                    ETHAN
          Bloody thou art, and bloody
          will be thy end.

                    SPEARING
          (Disgusted) Get 'em out of
          here.

As the GUARDS lead ETHAN and KAREN down the RV steps,
ETHAN elbows GUARD #2 in the groin.

GUARD #1 swings around to see what's happening.
KAREN'S foot smashes his face.

ETHAN and KAREN run.

Bullets WHIZ by.

THE BIG CHASE (Real street names and places are used
here):

EXT. CHATTANOOGA - NIGHT

MUSIC throughout the chase: "The Brazilian," an
instrumental by Genesis.

ETHAN and KAREN run across a road filled with people
peering at the devastation and approach a 7-11.

A jacked-up, F-350 pick-up truck pulls up, its
headlights on high beam.

The DRIVER, a construction worker, gets out, leaves
the truck running, and goes into the store.

INT./EXT. TRUCK - MOVING - NIGHT

ETHAN and KAREN steal the truck. ETHAN drives.

ETHAN and KAREN ROAR down Gun Barrel Road.

                    KAREN
          Do you really have Richard's
          heart?

                    ETHAN
          Yes.

                    KAREN
          And you really hear him? Feel
          him?

                    ETHAN
          Yes. Richard is *King* of my
          reality.

                    KAREN
          What does that mean exactly?

                    ETHAN
          It means he's driving.

KAREN smiles.

The truck zooms up on a line of traffic.

ETHAN crosses the double yellow line, passes several
cars.

In a curve, ETHAN passes a Taurus and meets an
oncoming semi.

ETHAN punches the gas and cuts the wheel to barely
escape a head-on. The rear truck bumper peels off the
bumper cover of the car.

A 1977, mint-condition Z-28 is now in the way.

ETHAN drives up a wheelchair ramp and takes the
sidewalk, passing up the Z-28, whose driver smiles
sadistically, and speeds up. It's a game.

A black FBI cruiser joins the race.

ETHAN slams into a large blue mailbox with the truck's
brush guard.

The mailbox sails through the air and lands on the
hood of the Z-28. Mail spills all over the street.

                    KAREN
          Now you've committed a
          felony.

                    ETHAN
          Thanks for pointing that out.

The FBI car zips through the mail, sideswipes the Z-
28.

ETHAN plows the truck back onto the road. A cruiser blocks his way at an intersection.

ETHAN smashes through that and turns onto Brianerd Road, a busy four-lane artery.

More cruisers join the chase.

ETHAN runs a red light and leaves more wreckage behind. This stalls the FBI cruisers, only now a city cop joins the chase.

ETHAN enters Missionary Ridge Tunnel.

                    ETHAN (CONT'D)
          Who the hell names things in
          this town?

In the tunnel lights, KAREN spots a lot of junk in the cab.

                    KAREN
          Oh. Chase toys.

KAREN rolls down her window and tosses out a spade, a 2x4, and a box of electrical stuff. The CITY COP loses control of his car avoiding these things and crashes.

                    KAREN (CONT'D)
          Who says you need a gun?

A STATE POLICE CRUISER is headed straight at the truck.

                    ETHAN
          A gun would be nice about
          now.

                    KAREN
          Looks like chicken for
          dinner, Honey.

At the last second the STATE POLICE cruiser veers into the wall. CRASH!

The FBI cruisers are gaining again.

ETHAN exits the tunnel and turns onto Main Street headed downhill and nearly airborne.

A banner over the street reads: WATER FEST * ROSS'S LANDING PARK: BOATS * JET SKIS * SAIL BOATS * BASS BUGGIES

                    KAREN (CONT'D)
          Why does Ross's Landing sound
          familiar?

                    ETHAN
          It's one of the places where
          the Trail of Tears began.

                    KAREN
          Now they sell bass buggies
          here?

                    ETHAN
          Yay, western expansion.

KAREN tosses a box of wood screws.

                    KAREN
          Screw you.²

An FBI car gets pelted, but there's little damage.

ETHAN SCREECHES onto Broad Street. An FBI car closes
in.

KAREN finds a power saw. Tosses it.

The saw lands blade up. The right front tire of
the cruiser strikes the saw. The teeth of the
blade bite into the tire.

The saw rolls up into the wheel well as the car
careens over it. The tire is ripped and the steering
is gone.

The cruiser smashes through the front window of the
"International Towing and Recovery Hall of Fame &
Museum" (actual place) and lands on the tow hooks of a
'37 Dodge tow truck.

                    KAREN
          I hope he has Triple A.

Floodlights from three police cars parked along
the street snap on.

SPEARING stands to one side with officers.

---

² Asst. Editor: Some of these jokes are too cheesy.
  Publisher: Not if the actors "under-act" the scene,
      then the cheese becomes part of the joke.
  Writer: I just want to be left alone.

The TRUCK runs over a spike strip.

                    ETHAN
          We *don't* have Triple A, so
          cut and run.

ETHAN and KAREN jump from the moving truck and
run toward a parking lot full of boats on
trailers for the Water Fest.

KAREN spots a 32-foot yacht on the back of a flatbed
trailer which is hitched to a semi.

A banner on the trailer proclaims the ship's name:
"Diamond in the Rough."

The ship lies at a 45-degree angle on starboard, its
keel and railing hang over the opposite sides of the
trailer. "Wide load."

POLICE and AGENTS swarm the parking lot.

                    KAREN
          This way. Let me drive. You
          never were good with a stick.

ETHAN and KAREN climb into the rig. She puts it in
gear.

                    ETHAN
          (Looking around the cab) Nice
          up-grade.

                    KAREN
          Thanks.

The DRIVER of the rig runs up yelling:

                    DRIVER
          What the hell are you doing?
          She isn't even strapped down
          now.

The truck creeps forward. The ship slips in its
props.

                    DRIVER (CONT'D)
          (To police) Hey. Over here!
          Somebody's stealing my truck!

POLICE and AGENTS arrive just as the truck starts
making its way across the parking lot - they then run
back for their cars.

KAREN steers the truck and ship onto 6th Street.

Two police cruisers whip into place to block the street. KAREN trashes them.

COPS start shooting but only hit the yacht.

Five FBI cars fall in behind in a slow chase.

6th Street becomes very steep.

Well up the street, KAREN shifts the truck into neutral.

The semi and trailer lurch to a stop for a very long pause. Then it all begins to roll backward.

Cruisers pile up trying to stop. The rig picks up speed.

KAREN stomps the brake pedal with both feet.

The air brakes HISS, the wheels all lock up, and the truck and trailer stop.

The MUSIC stops.

But -- the untethered ship sets sail off the back of the trailer and down the street.

> KAREN
> (Yelling out the window) Bon
> Voyage, Captain Spearing!

AGENTS flee their cars as the ship plows into them on its side.

The keel knocks off a fire hydrant. Water spews everywhere.

> ETHAN
> Well that went off without a
> hitch.

> KAREN
> Time for us to sail, too. But
> this whale is too obvious.

> ETHAN
> Beach it.

KAREN cuts the steering wheel slightly to the right, and they both jump out.

107

As KAREN and ETHAN flee, the rig rolls backwards again. The cab veers to the right, and the trailer journeys left.

The rig jackknifes, rolls over in a twisted heap, and knocks down a power pole.

Power lines break free and swing into the rushing water below.

KAREN and ETHAN vanish.

SPEARING is defeated. He looks over the mess then throws a tantrum.

END BIG CHASE

INT. FARMHOUSE - NIGHT

BEVERLY enters the house.

                    BEVERLY
          Ethan? Are you here?

BEVERLY sees the journal on the table. She sits and reads.

INT. BARN - NIGHT

BEVERLY enters with a bunch of carrots and approaches SOPHIA's stall. BEVERLY has been crying.

                    BEVERLY
          Oh Sophia. I think our ETHAN
          has lost his mind. What are
          we going to do girl, hmmm?

SOPHIA nibbles on a carrot. BEVERLY absently eats one. BEVERLY glances around the barn.

BEVERLY'S eyes fall on the old tractor. She sees track marks in the dirt and realizes its been moved recently. She walks over, scoots it out of the way, finds the money buried there.

                    BEVERLY (CONT'D)
          It's true? Oh my God, Ethan.
          What have you done? And just
          when I need you the most.
          What have you done?

BEVERLY cries.

EXT. CHATTANOOGA RESIDENTIAL AREA - NIGHT.

A police cruiser creeps down an old street with the
spotlight searching the shadows. The car leaves the
scene.

ETHAN and KAREN step out from behind some shrubs.

                    KAREN
          That's my ride over there.

ETHAN heads for a Lexus. KAREN walks to a VW hippie
bus. ETHAN realizes his mistake.

                    ETHAN
          You've got to be kidding me.

                    KAREN
          (Laughing) Just get over
          here.

KAREN steps into the central area of van, opens a
footlocker full of guns, ammo, and bomb materials.

                    ETHAN
          Not very hippie-ish, but I
          approve.

                    KAREN
          Thanks.

                    ETHAN
          But do you know where we're
          going?

                    KAREN
          The ETIC facilities. Spearing
          told me about them once, when
          we were dating. Before I met
          you - or Richard ...

                    ETHAN
          Where is it?

They close the side door and get into the van
themselves.

                    KAREN
          North-Central West Virginia.

                    ETHAN
          North? Central? West?

109

                    KAREN
          That's what they call the
          area.

KAREN starts the engine.

                    ETHAN
          So we're going to W. V. in a
          V. W.

                    KAREN
          You're a fast learner.

KAREN puts the VW in gear and pulls out.

EXT. CAMPSITE - NIGHT

ETHAN and KAREN sit on a blanket by a campfire, the VW
close by. KAREN studies the stars.

MUSIC comes from the VW radio: "Pocketful of Sunshine
(Only Butterflies)" by Natasha Bedingfield.

                    KAREN
          I wish it was a full moon
          tonight.

                    ETHAN
          In my heart the moon is
          always full.

ETHAN and KAREN smile at each other.

                    KAREN
          May I listen to it?

                    ETHAN
          Sure.

ETHAN unbuttons his shirt, reveals the scar on his
chest. KAREN gently places an ear over the scar,
listens.

                    KAREN
          Oh, how I've missed you, my
          love.

KAREN and ETHAN kiss and make love.

INT. BARN - DAWN

BEVERLY sits leaning against a post, the money scattered around her. She hasn't slept and has a 1000-yard stare.

BEVERLY shakes suddenly, closes her eyes a moment, then takes a deep breath. She pulls out her cell phone, dials.

> BEVERLY
> Yes, Dr. Young? This is Beverly Blake, Ethan's wife. (Beat) I need discreet medical advice. It involves Ethan, and, well it ... (Beat) Yes. This afternoon would be great. (Beat) Yes. Thank you so much, Dr. Young.

BEVERLY clicks off the phone.

> BEVERLY (CONT'D)
> (To herself). New heart, new start.

EXT. WEST VIRGINIA ROADS - MORNING

Shots of the VW van making its way across the New River Gorge Bridge and through other scenic WV places.

> KAREN (V.O.)
> ETIC is hidden in plain site, in the FBI Fingerprint Center. It occupies three floors, two of which are below ground. There are also several NASA facilities, high-tech companies, and national guard bases in the surrounding area. All of this is nestled in the out-of-the-way hills, but still close to highways and DC. The central purpose for these is to prepare for extraterrestrial contact and the possibility it will be hostile. The need for secrecy is paramount to national and global security.

EXT. FBI FINGERPRINT CENTER (A REAL PLACE) - DAY

TITLE CARD: FBI FINGERPRINT CENTER.

SECOND TITLE CARD: North-Central-West Virginia.

SHOT of ETIC truck backing into the building. It has an oversized load covered in white plastic.

NASIM and NORWICH watch their cargo carefully.

On a hill in the background, among some pine trees, ETHAN and KAREN watch through binoculars.

                    ETHAN
          The fence is electric and
          there are cameras everywhere.

                    KAREN
          Yeah, we may have to go in
          the front door.

                    ETHAN
          Have a plan?

                    KAREN
          An idea for one. And for our
          getaway.

KAREN examines a helicopter on the parking lot.

                    KAREN (CONT'D)
          Remember that abandoned
          concrete plant a couple miles
          back up the road?

                    ETHAN
          (Smiling). Gotcha.

INT. ETIC GREAT ROOM - DAY

The Great Room is about three stories high with a dome/cathedral ceiling:

A great round room, carved stone/washed in browns, grays, /and earth under a dome of /lights that spray patterns /like an electric spider spitting white silks.[3]

_____

[3] See entire poem in Appendix C.

112

An overhead crane lowers the UFO/Cocoon to a platform on the concrete floor.

The UFO is the size of a bus, basically cylindrical, and covered with various gadgets - all blackened and dirty.

Two ARMY SOLDIERS stand near-by with an ARMY JEEP.

NORWICH and NASIM gaze in wonder. NORWICH places her hand on it, **contact**.

> NORWICH
> And so it begins. HeartBeat-7 is a success. We finally have enough data to know where these are coming from.

NORWICH points to a place on the UFO. It looks like a plaque of some sort.

> NORWICH (CONT'D)
> There. That's where we begin cleaning.

INT. ETIC BROOM CLOSET - DAY

SPEARING sits down on an up-side-down bucket.

> SPEARING
> (To himself). ET's, transplanted people, angry women. All we need now is a Mexican Standoff.

SPEARING WHISTLES part of the theme to *The Good, The Bad, and The Ugly*, as he pulls a bag of white powder from his pocket.

ATTACK SCENE

MUSIC: "Are You Gonna Go My Way" by Lenny Kravitz

EXT. OLD, ORANGE CONCRETE MIXER - MOVING - DAY

CLOSE UP ON white dust blowing off the hood of an orange concrete truck.

INT. OLD, ORANGE CONCRETE MIXER - MOVING - DAY

MUSIC CONT.

ETHAN/RICHARD and KAREN have hot-wired a very old,
rattle-trap of a concrete mixer truck. The windows are
rolled down.

ETHAN/RICHARD and KAREN are dressed in black and
draped in guns and weapons. ETHAN sits in the
driver's seat.

                    ETHAN/RICHARD
          See. I'm fine with a stick
          shift.

                    KAREN
          But can you handle the
          controlled crash?

                    ETHAN/RICHARD
          Take you to school is what
          I'll do.

KAREN cocks an UZI.

INT./EXT. GATES OF FBI CENTER/CONCRETE MIXER CAB - DAY

MUSIC CONT.

The gates have low canopies and are narrow.

The concrete truck approaches, speeds up. A GATE GUARD
waves his hands to signal "slow down."

KAREN aims the UZI over his head and fires. The
windshield glass sprays out of the truck.

The mixer drum plows into the canopy. The canopy and
its supports cling to the truck.

GATE GUARDS stream out of a guardhouse, chase the
truck on foot.

As the truck nears the front of the main building:

                    KAREN
          NOW!

ETHAN cuts the steering wheel hard to the left. The
truck turns sideways, then slowly tips over.

KAREN and ETHAN unbuckle their seatbelts and crawl out
a window. ETHAN has a satchel of goodies on his
shoulder. Karen has rope and bands of ammo.

                    KAREN (CONT'D)
               You call that a controlled
               crash?

                    ETHAN
               Are you injured?

GATE GUARDS cautiously approach the truck. ETHAN and
KAREN take up positions behind the truck.

KAREN shoots the hat off a guard.

FIRE FIGHT.

INT. ETIC BROOM CLOSET - DAY

MUSIC CONT.

SPEARING truly "Chases the Dragon" using foil and a
straw to draw in the heroin vapors.

                    SPEARING
               Let us vaporize and chase the
               planets in Draco, so help us
               Ahab, may you rest in peace.

SPEARING starts to feel the rush.

ALARMS GO OFF.

                    SPEARING
               (Between bliss and fear).
               What the Fuck?

EXT. ETIC PARKING LOT - DAY

MUSIC CONT.

ETHAN and KAREN heave smoke grenades over the truck
for a smoke screen.

An FBI AGENT comes out of the front doors of the
center, takes a shot. ETAHN takes out the agent.

Other AGENTS are at the doors. ETHAN throws a
grenade.

ETHAN and KAREN run around the corner of the building
and try a side door. It's locked. ETHAN shoots the
lock. They enter the building.

INT. ETIC GREAT ROOM - DAY

MUSIC CONT.

ALARMS BLARING.

SPEARING rushes in, grabs an earpiece from a table,
and shoves it in his ear.

                    NORWICH
          What the hell is going on?

                    SPEARING
          Two people are storming the
          building.

PAUSE.

                    NORWICH
          You did not tell your
          girlfriend about ETIC, did
          you? (Beat). You idiot.

INT. CUBICLE HELL OF FBI CENTER - DAY

MUSIC CONT.

Fingerprint WORKERS cower under their desks as ETHAN
and KAREN fight off GUARDS and AGENTS. Hand-to-hand
combat. Thousands of fingerprint images flash by on
computer screens.

In the background, at a coffee cart, the HIPPIE/DUDE
from the opening scene, now in a robe, sandals, and
sunglasses, mixes a White Russian beverage - seemingly
oblivious to the utter chaos around him.

ETHAN picks up an earpiece from a dead agent, listens.

INT. GREAT ROOM - DAY

MUSIC CONT.

                    NORWICH
          Well. Where are they?

                    SPEARING
          They're in the office area
          right above us. They're
          fighting toward the east
          stairwell. That one over
          there.

SPEARING points to a stairwell door across the room.

                    NORWICH
          (To Troops). You two. Don't
          let anyone get through that
          door.

SPEARING backs away.

INT. CUBICLE HELL OF FBI CENTER - DAY

MUSIC CONT.

ETHAN hears Norwich's orders on the ear bud, motions
KAREN to go a different direction.

ETHAN and KAREN duck into an office. A SUIT cowers
under his desk. KAREN jumps up on the desk. ETHAN
glances at computer screen.

                    ETHAN
          (To Suit). Don't worry. Our
          prints are already in the
          system. Mine are under
          Hamlin, Richard. You're
          welcome.

ETHAN and KAREN disappear into the ductwork.

SHOTS of different places in the building, everything

117

quiet, everyone looking and listening. HIPPIE/DUDE
wanders around sipping his adult beverage.

INT. GREAT ROOM - DAY

MUSIC CONT.

                    NORWICH
          Where'd they go?

                    SPEARING
          Nobody has eyes on them.

PAUSE.

                    NASIM
          I thought it was the aliens
          we're supposed to worry
          about.

                    NORWICH
          This is intolerable.

ETHAN appears in the background, creeps up behind
SPEARING. He now has a micro-camera on his head,
filming the scene.

ETHAN pulls a wired block of C4 explosive from his
satchel. It is taped to a pair of handcuffs. Next
ETHAN pulls out an Remote Control detonator.

Finally ETHAN draws a knife from an ankle sheath so
that the switch and knife handle are both in his right
hand.

ETHAN presses the switch and thrusts the knife to
SPEARING'S throat.

                    SPEARING
          What the ...

                    ETHAN
          Easy big boy.

ETHAN slaps the cuffs and explosives onto one of
SPEARING's wrists.

EVERYONE in the room turns to see ETHAN and SPEARING.

                         ETHAN
            Nobody move. Good. As you can
            see, Willy here has a bomb.
            I have the detonator. Button
            already pressed. Shoot me,
            and he's history.   Got it?

                         NORWICH
            Got it, Cowboy.

ETHAN hits a button on a consol. The ALARMS stop.

Suddenly a vent grate falls from the ceiling, followed
by a rope. KAREN slides down the rope and lands on
the UFO.

MUSIC STOPS when KAREN's feet hit the UFO.

                         NORWICH (CONT'D)
            Oh. And here's his cow wench.

KAREN cocks the UZI and aims it at NORWICH.

                         NORWICH
            Typical. And what do the two
            of you hope to get out of all
            this?

                         ETHAN
            First - we want ol' Willy
            here dead.

                         NORWICH
            Fine. Take him.

                         SPEARING
            WHAT!?

                         ETHAN
            But then we realized how
            important all this is and how
            our government is shielding
            us from the truth. That's
            why I'm filming, by the way.

                         KAREN
            You knew this thing was
            coming. You knew the
            trajectory. How could you let
            over two hundred people die?

                         NORWICH
            National Security.

                         119

                    ETHAN
          Bullshit. Tell that to the
          families.

                    NORWICH
          Come look at this.

NORWICH leads ETHAN to the freshly cleaned plaque on
the UFO. ETHAN studies it. KAREN hovers above.

                    ETHAN
          What is it?

                    NORWICH
          We're not sure yet, but it
          seems to be some sort of
          galactic map with information
          about its senders. It's
          similar to the one we put on
          Pioneer 10, the first
          spacecraft to leave our solar
          system. This is a probe.

                    ETHAN
          Okay. But national security?
          Really?

                    NORWICH
          Look here on the right side.
          This appears to be a map of
          our solar system. This line
          is the path this probe
          followed.

                    ETHAN
          So?

                    KAREN
          So that means the life form
          that sent this isn't just on
          a fishing trip. They know
          we're here. They are reaching
          out.

                    NORWICH
          Reaching out or - planning to
          take over. What if they see
          us as their Manifest Destiny?

ETHAN gazes at the map, places his hand on it,
contact.

                    ETHAN
          (To himself). But there is
          intelligent life out there.
          That much we know for sure.

PAUSE. ETHAN walks along the craft, stops at the large
glass lens in the nose of the UFO.

                    ETHAN (CONT'D)
          And what's inside?

                    NORWICH
          We don't know. There's no
          sign of biological life -
          yet.

                    KAREN
          (Still standing on top) Maybe
          it's a Red Tesla Roadster.

EVERYONE stares up at KAREN in
disgusted silence. Then:

                    KAREN
          Sorry. Just a joke. You know.
          WOW. Tough room.

                    ETHAN
          (To Norwich) People deserve
          to know about this.

                    NORWICH
          No, they don't. They deserve
          no such thing. Besides the
          massive chaos that would
          accompany this news, which
          really doesn't concern me,
          this planet is about to turn
          into a cesspool. We are dead
          in the water.

                    ETHAN
          What?

                    NORWICH
          Earth is fucked, and this
          probe may hold our ticket to
          human survival. But I sure
          don't plan to save seven
          billion grubby-nosed humans
          to fight and spread ignorance
          to the rest of the galaxy.
          Only a few of us enlightened
          souls are taking this

                    121

opportunity to forge
something better for the
future of human civilization.

                    ETHAN
(Pointing at the camera on
his head). We'll just have to
see about that, won't we?

                    NORWICH
At least you know your place
(looks over at Spearing),
unlike some people.

                    SPEARING
(To Norwich) But I thought -
I though I was part of the
plan.

                    NORWICH
Like you ever really had a
chance. But I do appreciate
your investment, William.
Truly. I shall name some
building or something after
you. It's the least we can
do after your untimely death
- today.

                    SPEARING
(To Karen) Karen, talk some
sense into this man. Get
this bomb off of me. It's
not too late for us.

                    KAREN
Sorry, William. You do kinda
need to die for your sins.

                    NORWICH
(To Karen) Oh. You're dying
today, too. (BEAT) You know
what they say about revenge.
I hope you two dug plenty of
graves.

                    SPEARING
But Karen, I love you.

                    KAREN
Oh, Honey. That's just the
explosives talking.

                    ETHAN
          (To Karen) I think it's time
          to go, dear. We're
          overstaying our welcome.

ETHAN walks to a console and pushes a button. The
huge garage door opens.

Outside, a small battalion of AGENTS and GUARDS have
their guns fixed on the door opening.

ETHAN holds up the detonator for them to see.

                    ETHAN (CONT'D)
          You first, Spearing.

KAREN jumps down from the UFO.

                    KAREN
          The rest of you stay here
          until you hear the helicopter
          take off. Or it's bye-bye
          Spearing and anyone near him.

EXT. FBI CENTER PARKING LOT - EVENING

KAREN, ETHAN, and SPEARING walk out the garage
doors and up the driveway to the parking lot.

GUARDS and AGENTS back away from SPEARING.

KAREN and ETHAN get into the helicopter.

ETHAN sticks the hand with the detonator out the
window for all to see.

KAREN fires up the engine.

INT. GREAT ROOM - EVENING

NORWICH hears the engine and walks over to the Army
Jeep.

NORWICH throws back a cover on the back of the Jeep
and pulls out a surface-to-air missile and launcher.

                    123

EXT. PARKING LOT/HELICOPTER - EVENING

Just as the helicopter lifts off the pad, NORWICH
appears and takes aim at it with the missile.

                    KAREN
          We have a problem.

KAREN puts the chopper in a menacing nose-down
position.

ETHAN waves the detonator.

PEOPLE move even farther from SPEARING.

                    SPEARING
          (To Norwich) (SHOUTING over
          chopper noise) No! Put it
          down. Don't shoot Karen.

                    NORWICH
          (SHOUTING To Spearing) Fuck
          off.

NASIM appears at NORWICH'S side with a bullhorn.

                    NASIM
          Put the chopper back down.
          We can talk.

SPEARING looks in the back of an FBI cruiser parked
near him. He opens the door, reaches in, and pulls out
a fully automatic rifle.

SPEARING aims it at NORWICH.

                    SPEARING (SHOUTING)
          I said let them go!

NORWICH and NASIM look to see SPEARING with the bomb
and a gun.

NASIM raises her hands.

GRAND PAUSE

A big guns version of a MEXICAN STANDOFF.

                    ETHAN
          (In Ethan's voice) All I ever
          really wanted was to be left
          alone.

ETHAN and RICHARD YELL like crazed soldiers in a battlefield charge.

Then:

ETHAN lets go of the detonator just as SPEARING opens fire.

SPEARING becomes a red vapor with bullets flying out of it.

NASIM is hit by several bullets.

NORWICH is shot in the leg just after she fires the missile

ETHAN and KAREN die as the chopper blows up.

NORWICH is the last woman standing.

FADE TO BLACK

TITLE CARD: 18 MONTHS LATER

INT. FARMHOUSE ENTRYWAY - DAY

KNOCKING at the door. BEVERLY opens the door to reveal SISTER RITA.

> BEVERLY
> Sister Rita. Thank you for coming.

SISTER RITA enters.

> SISTER RITA
> Thank you for having me. I had wondered how things worked out.

BEVERLY and SISTER RITA move to the living room.

INT. FARMHOUSE LIVING ROOM - DAY

ANGLE ON: Photo of BEVERLY and DOCTOR YOUNG happily smiling - together.

BEVERLY and SISTER RITA sit.

                    BEVERLY
          You said I was in for some
          big changes, but you didn't
          say how big.

                    SISTER RITA
          I didn't want to alarm you,
          dear. Besides I wasn't
          entirely sure of my vision.

                    BEVERLY
          I understand. So you've read
          the copy of Ethan's journal
          that I sent you?

                    SISTER RITA
          Yes. Thank you for sharing.

                    BEVERLY
          You're welcome.

There is a muffled NOISE elsewhere in the house.

                    BEVERLY (CONT'D)
          Well that didn't take long.
          He's awake. Would you like to
          see him?

                    SISTER RITA
          Yes. Yes I would.

INT.   NURSERY - DAY

BEVERLY leads SISTER RITA into the room, toward a
crib.

BLAKE, a baby boy of about 10 months, is sitting in
the crib and playing with a plastic hammer as if
discovering a tool [ENGLISH TEACHERS, this is an
allusion to *2001: A Space Odyssey*].

                    SISTER RITA
          My, he's so handsome.

                    BEVERLY
          I named him Ethan Richard
          Blake. I call him Blake.
          (Beat) I conceived the night
          after Ethan killed the drug
          dealers in Columbus.

                    SISTER RITA
          And you think ...

                         BEVERLY
                After all, Ethan couldn't
                have children ...

SISTER RITA touches the baby's soft hair. BLAKE
smiles.

                         BEVERLY
                Then two weeks ago Blake did
                something that convinced me
                entirely.

                         SISTER RITA
                What?

BEVERLY leans over and kisses BLAKE on the head.

                         BEVERLY
                (To Blake) Honey? Could you
                tell Mommy and Sister Rita
                what you've been saying?

BLAKE looks into the camera with a smile. Then he
opens his little mouth, and in a small, sing-song
voice:

                         BLAKE
                Vengeance is mine. I will
                survive. I will destroy them
                all.

FREEZE FRAME on little BLAKE'S innocent face.

Cue the haunting, opening strains of The Rolling
Stones' "Gimme Shelter (I'm just a kiss away)."

ROLL CREDITS

When "Gimme Shelter" ends, follow it with Billy
Thorpe's "Children of the Sun."

POST CREDITS BONUS SCENE:

INT. ETIC GREAT ROOM - NIGHT

The UFO/COCOON sits alone in the dimly lit room.

We HEAR a door CREAK open and close.

HIPPIE/DUDE enters, in bathrobe, sandals, short pants.
He carries a white Russian beverage and a folding
chair.

DUDE comes to within a few feet of the UFO, sets up
his chair, and sits down.

Once he is settled, he pulls a small version of the
UFO/Cocoon - the one he presumably picked up in the
opening scene of the movie - from his robe pocket.

He aims it like a flashlight at the "Mother Ship" and
presses a button. The Mother Ship/Cocoon lights up
with colorful and blinking lights.

The big glass lens in its nose glows blue, as does the
lens on the one in his hand.

With a SWOOSH and spurt of steam, a hatch opens on the
Mother Ship.

Hundreds of blue, bio-mechanical butterflies emerge,
and, flying gently, they fill the GREAT ROOM.

Lastly, a GOLD BUTTERFLY exits the ship. It flutters
about for a moment, then hovers near the HIPPIE.

He smiles and extends a hand with his index finger
out.

The GOLD BUTTERFLY lands on the finger.

The HIPPY stares at it with joy and laughs.

                    HIPPY/DUDE
          Welcome to your new home, my
          friend. Welcome home.

          T H E   E N D

APPENDIX A
Fantasy Cast

A general rule of screenwriting, especially for unknowns like me, is to NEVER write with specific actors in mind. And, I didn't, because writers never get to pick the actors. That's the job of the casting director, director, and producers. But this is not a screenplay. It's a SCREEN BOOK, and I'm making the rules!

Henceforth, be it known that writers of SCREEN BOOKS are expected to add an appendix labeled "Fantasy Cast." They are to imagine whom they wish to play various roles and explain their picks.

Here are mine in (roughly) the order of appearance.

Richard Hamlin: Hugo Weaving (He has the intensity of a bitter FBI agent plus a cool voice to play with as Richard and Ethan merge).

Stanley: Bruce Willis (Finally! He dies hard, and in the first 10 minutes to boot! It's a win/win.)

Dreads: Bahram Radan (The Iranian Brad Pitt. But would he grow the needed hair-ware?)

Ahab: Maz Jobrani (Known for comedy, but has the attitude).

William Spearing: Phil Collins (It is imperative to have an 80's rock star with a British accent somewhere in a film full of rock music. Chase "The Brazilian," Phil. I mean, Mr. Collins.).

Ethan Blake: Adam Beach (my favorite Native American Actor).

Beverly Blake: Melissa Shepherd (a great friend and fine actress who deserves a shot).

Dr. Tanner: Pat Conner (my mentor on Chaucer manuscript studies in graduate school). I saw him act out much of *Beowulf* in Anglo-Saxon class - IN OLD ENGLISH! Now he has a second career as a film and stage actor).

Dr. Michael Young: The executive producer's son's step-sister's brother-in-law (Even the best of movies have some nepotism).

Anesthesiologist: Sean Kach (My cousin).

Sister Rita/Dr. Deborah Norwich: Catherine Zeta Jones (I am secretly in love with her).

Nasim: Catherine Bell (Yes. She is Persian).

Allyson: Kaley Cuoco (*The Big Bang Theory* must be represented somewhere in this mischievous sci-fi flick).

Karen: Tristan Mays (Attitude and looks. No wonder Richard/Ethan loved/love her).

Uncle John: Richard Ray Whitman (See him practically steal the movie in *Neither Wolf Nor Dog*).

Granny: Tantoo Cardinal (Need I say more? A Native woman with grit and grace is a granny by default).

Bookshop Keeper: John Irving (An author with attitude minding a Bookstore? Yes, Please. [Great work as the referee in *Garp*, John]).

Hippy Dude Making a White Russian: Me (Write the part you were born to play).

Baby Blake, AKA Little Richard. It is my sincere hope that Lady Gaga and Bruno Mars produce a love child at just the right time for my movie.

APPENDIX B
The HeartBeat Playlist

Sweet Emotion - Aerosmith
The Main Monkey Business - Rush
Making a Noise - Robbie Robertson
Total Eclipse of the Heart - Bonnie Tyler
Brain Damage - Pink Floyd

Every Breath You Take - The Police
Jump - Van Halen
Sorrow - Pink Floyd
Fantasy - Aldo Nova
The Groove is in the Heart - Dee Lite

The Brazilian - Genesis
Pocketful of Sunshine - Natasha Bedingfield
Are You Gonna Go My Way - Lenny Kravitz
Gimme Shelter - The Rolling Stones
Children of the Sun - Billy Thorpe

This poem was inspired by the 1993 song and official video, "Are You Gonna Go My Way?" by Lenny Kravitz, arguably the last great rock song ever written. The Great Room of ETIC came out of my dreams and nightmares. This video captures something of what my brain visions look like.

My newest addiction:

a snake wrapped around
my body, shooting me up
with dopamine from its fangs,
jacking up my brain without pills.

The venom milked in
a great round room, carved stone
washed in browns, grays,
and earth under a dome of
lights that spray patterns
like an electric spider
spitting white silks. A place
I visit in my dreams
thrown thru a dark glass canvas.
Watch it now. A drummer with
intense precision is balanced on
the thinnest line of time possible.
LK follows her path only to
draw *me* out of my abyss
and toss me onto the
dirty concrete floor,
alive and closer to myself.

We are ringed by dancers who are
vaguely aware of their sublimity.
A few brave ones fly & swim in the
gentle sea -- undefeated, resonant,
repurposed as music from the stars.

This is my world too,
and I just wanted a few
of you to know that.

ACKNOWLEDGEMENTS

Deborah Allen, The Black Dog Writers, Brian Bellomy,
Cindy Crawford, Beverly Delidow, James Emmert,
Sandy Farrar, The Guyandotte Poets Society,
Hayley Mitchell Haugen, Tom Jones, Sandee Lloyd,
Bernadette Rene Reynolds, Melissa Shepherd,
Darian Spurlock, Art Stringer, Dwayne Walters,
Clark and Marlene Wolfe (May They Rest In Peace),
And my daughter, Katie Wolfe.